BAD WEDDING

BILLIONAIRE'S CLUB #9

ELISE FABER

BAD WEDDING
BY ELISE FABER
Newsletter sign-up

This is a work of fiction. Names, places, characters, and events are fictitious in every regard. Any similarities to actual events and persons, living or dead, are purely coincidental. Any trademarks, service marks, product names, or named features are assumed to be the property of their respective owners, and are used only for reference. There is no implied endorsement if any of these terms are used. Except for review purposes, the reproduction of this book in whole or part, electronically or mechanically, constitutes a copyright violation.

BILLIONAIRE'S CLUB

Bad Night Stand

Bad Breakup

Bad Husband

Bad Hookup

Bad Divorce

Bad Fiancé

Bad Boyfriend

Bad Blind Date

Bad Wedding

Bad Engagement

BILLIONAIRE'S CLUB CAST OF CHARACTERS

Heroes and Heroines:

Abigail Roberts (*Bad Night Stand*) — founding member of the Sextant, hates wine, loves crocheting

Jordan O'Keith (*Bad Night Stand*) — Heather's brother, former owner of RoboTech

Cecilia (CeCe) Thiele (*Bad Breakup*) — former nanny to Hunter, talented artist

Colin McGregor (*Bad Breakup*) — Scottish duke, owner of McGregor Enterprises

Heather O'Keith (*Bad Husband*) — CEO of RoboTech, Jordan's sister

Clay Steele (*Bad Husband*) — Heather's business rival, CEO of Steele Technologies

Kay (*Bad Date*) — romance writer, hates to be stood up

Garret Williams (*Bad Date*) — former rugby player

Rachel Morris (*Bad Hookup*) — Heather's assistant, super-powers include being ultra-organized

Sebastian (Bas) Scott (Bad Hookup) — Devon Scott's brother, Clay's assistant

Rebecca (Bec) Darden (Bad Divorce) — kickass lawyer, New York roots

Luke Pearson (Bad Divorce) — Southern gentleman, CEO Pearson Energies

Seraphina Delgado (Bad Fiancé) — romantic to the core, looks like a bombshell, but even prettier on the inside

Tate Connor (Bad Fiancé) — tech genius, scared to be burned by love

Lorelai (Bad Text) — drunk texts don't make her happy

Logan Smith (Bad Text) — former military, sometimes drunk texts are for the best

Kelsey Scott (Bad Boyfriend) — Bas and Devon's sister, engineer at RoboTech, brilliant

Tanner Pearson (Bad Boyfriend) — Bas and Devon's childhood friend, photographer

Trix Donovan (Bad Blind Date) — Heather's sister, Jordan's half-sister, nurse who worked in war zones, poverty-stricken areas, and abroad for almost a decade

Jet Hansen (Bad Blind Date) — a doctor Trix worked with

Molly Miller (Bad Wedding) — owner of Molly's, a kickass bakery in San Francisco

Jackson Davis (Bad Wedding) — Molly's ex-fiancé

Additional Characters:

George O'Keith — Jordan's dad
Hunter O'Keith — Jordan's nephew
Bridget McGregor — Colin's mom
Lena McGregor — Colin's sister

Bobby Donovan — Heather's half and Trix's full brother
Frances and Sugar Delgado — Sera's parents
Devon Scott — Kels and Bas's brother
Becca Scott — Kels and Bas's sister in law

ONE

Molly

SHE CHECKED the bread that was proofing in the oven, not opening the door and risking a disruption of those teeny bubbles that were still forming, but peering through the glass rectangle on the oven door and making sure those pale globes of bread were rising as they should.

Her homemade rolls were a top-seller, usually gone before ten in the morning.

That was because they were delicious, if she said so herself.

And she *did* say so, she supposed, snorting at her pun.

But puns were all she had at zero-dark-thirty in the morning. Zero-dark-thirty, otherwise known as four A.M. It was a stupid hour to be up and about, but she owned a bakery and that meant she had to get up early. Molly's—yes, she was egotistical enough to own a place named after herself, though in fairness, she hadn't come up with the name—served breakfast and lunch, with a limited staff and menu for dinner.

That limited menu meant she didn't have to work at dinnertime.

A good thing, too. Otherwise, she might as well live at the restaurant.

And while she loved Molly's, she also loved having a life.

Not that you've had much of that lately.

True.

But owning a restaurant in a big city was difficult, and even more difficult was to *keep* owning it. Molly had investors to reimburse, loans to pay off, wages to cover, and supplies to purchase.

So, that meant filling in if her evening cook had a date or got sick or worked only five days a week. Okay, so if she were being truthful, that meant she all but lived at the bakery an average of four days out of said week.

But that was better than seven, so there was that.

Seeing that the rolls were doing well, Molly turned back to the counter to finish up the rest of her prep. She had to toast some walnuts, get the *mise en place* ready for her soups—which were basically fancy words to say she was chopping up the onions and carrots, celery and potatoes and peppers, measuring stocks and creams, roasting cobs of corn.

Her rolls dinged, and she grabbed them out, switching them to the preheated oven, doing a little dance of adding another baking sheet in to proof, pulling out a tray of croissants that were done from a different oven and replacing them with peach turnovers. She packed up the *mise en place* and stored them in the fridge, then prepped several bowls of muffin batter—today would be lemon poppy seed, peaches and cream, blueberry, and double chocolate.

Once the turnovers were done, she divided the muffin batter into various tins then began rocking through baking them off while stocking the glass case next to the counter. It was a familiar routine. Her doors opened at five, but that was mostly for her few straggler early birds, and that wasn't typically more than five or six people, so she mostly let the first bell tinkling above the door let her know when she needed to pull her ass out of the kitchen. Which meant that she had to have the first batch of everything baked off before that. After her first employees clocked in at six-thirty, she could stay in the kitchen like she preferred.

Baking was her favorite.

The people weren't bad either. She loved getting to know them, to see them change, their lives grow full and happy, their kids get older. She loved *feeding* people, even if they weren't regulars.

There was absolutely nothing better than seeing someone's happy smile when they bit into something tasty.

Speaking of, the bell above the door tinkled as her first customer of the day strode into the bakery.

"I'll be with you in a second," she called, continuing to fill the case with lemon muffins.

"I did always love to see you like this."

Molly jumped, eyes shooting up.

It had been so long since she'd heard that voice.

I love taking bites out of you.

It had rumbled back then, too, rasping along her skin, skating down her spine, and making her shiver.

The first man she'd baked for.

The man who'd given her the money to open this place.

The one who'd *named* it.

And the one who'd left her at the altar. In the white dress. With the venue booked. With the caterer and the DJ set up. With the guests packing the pews on both sides of the isle.

Jackson Davis.

Jackson *Fucking* Davis.

"Jackson," she murmured and slid the back of the case closed.

"I'm back, honey."

She'd regret her actions later, but in that moment, with the memories of the full church and the people and their pitying expressions and *this man*. Not. Fucking. Showing. Up.

Molly snapped.

She threw the baking sheet at his head.

TWO

Jackson

IN FAIRNESS, he used to react faster.

His Molly seemed sweet and kind and levelheaded to the rest of the world, but with him, she always had a slice of fire.

He'd ducked a cookie sheet or twenty in their years together, but he'd been too long out of practice, too long away to remember how quickly she could launch that rectangle of steel, how it could unfailingly fly in perfect rotation toward his head.

Then it was there, inches away.

Jackson ducked at the last second, so the sheet glanced off his shoulder instead of his face.

Ouch. That was going to leave a bruise.

"Oh, my God," Molly said, hands coming up to cover the horrified expression she wore.

That was new.

The horrified reaction.

She never used to feel any remorse for losing her temper, for launching a sheet in his direction or cursing him out. For one, he always moved well before the sheet came close. For two, he always deserved her reaction.

He'd *curated* her reaction—poked and prodded and needled until she snapped.

Because there was something about seeing Molly pissed, watching the flush crawl over her cheeks, seeing her pale green eyes fill with sparks. She was beautiful normally, but she was absolutely stunning when she was pissed.

Not to mention her being pissed was usually trailed by angry sex.

And angry sex with Molly was the best.

Although . . . he didn't think angry sex was going to be on the plate with her today. Her hands dropped away from her face, those sparks faded away, and her pretty green eyes went damp.

"What the fuck, Jackson Davis?" she said. "What. The. Fuck?"

Then she spun on one heel and disappeared through the swinging door.

He stood there for a moment, staring after her, his heart hurting from the sight of her tears, regret a jagged and icy knife in his gut. He should have leveled with her from the second he'd found out, shouldn't have . . . done a lot of things.

Jackson sighed, shoved a hand through his hair.

He'd fucked up good.

Never let it be said that he didn't give it his all.

The bell above the door dinged and after a few seconds, he heard Molly's voice trail out of the back. "I'll be right out!"

Warm. As sweet as her cinnamon rolls and twice as calorie-laden. Or at least, that was how it had always felt to him. She just had to speak, and he was filled to the brim.

And he'd ruined that.

Fucking hell.

It was just after six in the morning. The case next to the register was full of various breakfast treats—croissants and muffins, fruit-filled Danishes, even a row of immaculately decorated flower cookies, the brightly-colored frosting punctuated with carefully placed sparkling sprinkles.

He knew she'd probably placed them with tweezers.

Because if there was one thing Molly was good at, it was caring about the details.

He'd once been one of those details.

Molly pushed through the door, another tray in her hands, her formerly askew ponytail carefully straightened and secured. She set the tray on the stainless-steel counter behind the case and smiled.

Not at him.

At the man who'd just walked through the door.

Fuck, Jackson didn't like that at all—her smiling at other men, even men who were well over seventy, had barely enough hair to cover an inch above each ear, and hobbled slowly in with a cane.

But he'd fucked up.

So, he didn't have a right to feel anything about her smiles.

"Ronnie," she said, still smiling, her eyes sliding deliberately past him, as though Jackson were nothing more than a piece of furniture, and an ugly one at that. "You want the usual?"

"Mornin', beautiful," Ronnie said then pointed at Jackson. "This young man was here first."

Molly smiled, though this time it was tinged with ice. "Oh, I've already helped him plenty." She tilted her head toward the windows. "Go sit at your table. I'll bring out your muffin and coffee."

"Black," Ronnie said.

"With only a half a pound of sugar," Molly added with

wink. "I know, honey. I'll warm you up a lemon poppy seed to go with it."

"You always know how to treat a guy." Ronnie put a five on the counter. "I wish I was forty years younger so I could marry you. Any man would be lucky to call you his wife." Then he grinned and made his halting way over to what was apparently *his* table, a small round top tucked into one corner.

It did not escape Jackson's notice that there was already a newspaper carefully laid there. One that Ronnie apparently expected, because he sat down and immediately got to reading.

It also did not escape Jackson's notice that Molly had stopped breathing.

That her face had paled, and pain had crawled across her eyes.

Because he'd once been the man who'd been lucky enough to marry Molly.

Fuck.

"Sweet—"

Her eyes flashed to his, hurt disappearing behind a mask of anger. "I think I made it clear when I sent you the paperwork. I don't want anything to do with you. Not now. Not *ever*." She bent, sliding open the back of the case and pulling out a muffin. Her movements were efficient, practiced, but wooden, and he knew she'd done the same thing a thousand times before.

She'd done the same dance many times over while hurting.

Because *he'd* hurt her.

Jackson didn't speak until she came back behind the counter. "Molly—"

Her head whipped up, but this time there wasn't hurt or anger on her face. Instead, it was determination and, fuck, he liked that expression even more than sparking furious eyes. "If you want more money," she said. "I'll find it. But I want you out of this business, Jackson."

Yeah, he was reading that loud and clear.

He'd gotten the papers the day before, couriered to his office, placed unceremoniously on his desk by his assistant, and they'd fucking pissed him off. An emotion he didn't have one right to feel about the situation, since it was entirely of his making, and yet, one he was furious about anyway.

What right did Molly have to cut this last tie between them? What fucking right?

Every right. She had *every* right. He knew that. He got that. He—

Couldn't bear to actually let her go.

A fucking joke considering he was the one who'd pulled the plug on their wedding, but also the truth.

Which is why he said, "I'm not going to let you buy me out," when he probably should have told her that he would sign whatever papers she wanted if she would only give him another chance.

But that wasn't his style.

Jackson wasn't altruistic. He wasn't good. He was selfish.

And he wanted Molly.

Green eyes sparked fire at his words, lush lips that fit perfectly against his flattened out, a muscle in her jaw ticked. She sucked in a breath, opened her mouth, and—

The bell jingled.

They both turned and watched a trio of men in suits walk through the door. Then the bell sounded again as another customer slipped inside. And then another. And another. They approached the counter, anticipation on their faces.

To talk to Molly. To eat her delicious food. To just soak in the warmth of her presence.

Jackson knew the feeling. He'd been stifling that urge for years.

Only he'd gotten really good at pretending he wasn't ruled

by those urges, that he didn't need the woman standing on the other side of the counter, her unruly hair escaping her ponytail, her curves unhidden even beneath the shapeless pastel pink apron she wore, the scent of all the delicious things she conjured up in the magical kitchen of hers surrounding him.

But he *did* need her.

He just didn't know how in the hell he was going to make amends for what he'd done.

THREE

Molly

SHE LEANED CAREFULLY to the side, peering through the round window at the top of the swinging door that led from the kitchen to the front of house, searching to see if it was safe.

It wasn't.

Jackson was still there.

When the morning rush had begun, he'd stepped away from the counter and she'd thought he would leave.

Thanked the baking gods that he wouldn't continue to darken her doorstep.

But instead of leaving, he'd picked up the plate with the lemon and poppy seed muffin she'd heated, snagged the coffee she'd poured and then dumped about a gallon of sugar into, and carried both over to Ronnie's table.

Now they were talking.

It had been nearly two hours. Jeanine, her morning shift cashier had come in, facilitating Molly's escape back into the kitchen. Ronnie had gone, the newspaper she left for him every morning folded carefully and tucked under one arm.

And Jackson remained.

Suit jacket off and draped over the back of his chair. Phone out, alternating between typing on it and placing it up to his ear and speaking into it. Yes, she could imagine the velvet rasp of his voice, practically feel it caressing her skin.

So many good times.

So much love.

And then . . . nothing.

He'd ghosted her to an insane degree, disappearing the morning of the wedding. His parents hadn't known where he'd gone, and neither had his groomsmen. She'd spent the day calling hospitals, organizing search parties, and driving the road between the hotel and the venue, looking for him or any sign of an accident. Eventually, she'd gone to the police department and filed a missing person report.

Then had received a phone call an hour later, asking her to come down to the station. She'd been panicked, on the verge of a nervous breakdown the whole way, thinking something horrible had happened to him. But then she'd been led into a room at the department, and Jackson had been standing there, whole and safe and . . . she'd run to him, thrown herself into his arms. *God.* She'd never forgot the humiliation of what had come next. The brusque way he'd set her away from him, his normally warm chocolate eyes having turned frozen and fierce.

"You have to stop, or I'll file a restraining order."

A restraining order.

While she'd stood there, heart shattering into tiny pieces, head spinning from his sudden transformation—her loving and devoted fiancé had turned into this cold and unfeeling monster —he'd calmly threatened her with a restraining order.

Calmly threatened.

Those two words shouldn't go together.

And yet, they did.

So, she'd gathered herself, lifted her chin, straightened her shoulders, steadied her voice, all while her heart was still breaking, and had slipped the ring off her finger.

The metal against metal sound of the band hitting the stainless-steel table had stayed with her for a long time. Because there had been a finality in the noise, a final nail in the coffin of what she'd always understood deep down in some dark corner of her mind was going to come. Jackson would leave her.

She'd known that.

She just . . . hadn't expected it to be on her wedding day.

Molly had left that tiny fluorescent-lit room and gone back to the apartment she shared with Jackson to find his things had been cleared out in the hour she'd been gone, a note scrawled in his handwriting left on the counter.

> *Lease paid up. Money in your bank account. Call this*
> *number when you need more.*
> *415-555-6979*
> *-J*

She could admit now that was the moment she'd fully lost it. Her purse had hit the floor, dumping its contents everywhere. Her keys she'd launched across the room, leaving a huge dent in the wall. Her cell . . . well, she'd launched it hard enough to probably tear through the sheetrock and fly into the unit next door, but thankfully her aim was off, and it rebounded off the couch and dropped to the floor, ending up functional, albeit with a broken screen.

Functional but broken.

Yeah, look her up in the dictionary and that would be the perfect definition.

And after all of that, the being left at the altar, the panic and worry of the day, the unceremonious dumping, she'd been left with a wedding to dismantle, gifts to return, venders to pay . . . and been threatened with a restraining order.

Because that was Molly's life.

In hindsight, she could see it was for the best.

She'd been on the precipice of giving up on Molly's. It was too much work for too little reward, and she'd wanted to start a family. There was no reason she should be working the hours she'd been working when Jackson had the means to easily take care of them both.

In the end, Molly's had been a godsend.

Because she hadn't used the money he'd left in her account. Because she'd been too hurt and angry and upset to accept being bought off. And because it had given her the strength to transform from an insecure girl into a strong woman who knew her worth.

She'd packed her stuff that evening then moved it and herself out of the apartment the following morning, living in her office in the bakery until she could afford her own apartment, paid with her own money.

She'd become someone she could be proud off.

A capable businesswoman, a kind human being, a kickass baker.

Not a weak female who'd just roll over and be whatever Jackson wanted her to be.

And while she blamed him for leaving, for hurting her in such a dramatic and unnecessary way, part of her also felt grateful, because she was a different person today than she'd been four years before. Because she was a better, stronger person.

"Then why are you here hiding in the kitchen instead of dealing with the man?" she muttered to herself.

Because she might be stronger, but she wasn't immune to all that was Jackson Davis.

The voice that made her stomach dip, the body she'd known

so intimately, the memories of all the wonderful things they'd shared.

It filled her with *so* much longing.

Hence her hiding.

"Damn," she muttered and sucked in a breath, knowing she needed to go out there and deal with him. The rush had died down, the cases needed to be refilled, she needed to give Jeanine her first break, and she needed to get this conversation over with Jackson—

The timer for her final pan of rolls dinged.

Thank the baking gods.

Couldn't have that conversation right now. She had rolls to pull out, more pastries to bake, Jeanine to give a break, soup to get simmering. Jackson Davis would just have to wait.

Of course, what she didn't take into account was that Jackson didn't much like waiting.

FOUR

Jackson

HE'D SPENT the last hours biding his time.

Well, biding his time along with putting a few things in place. The reason he'd called off his wedding four years ago hadn't mysteriously disappeared, so he needed to put a few measures in place.

He hadn't had the means then.

But he had them now.

What he needed to consider was if those means were worth the risk of what they might bring into Molly's life.

His cell buzzed with a call, but the door Molly had disappeared behind after her employee had arrived swung open at the same moment, and he immediately forget about the phone, about his reasons for leaving, about his current means. Jackson could think of *nothing* except for how much he wanted Molly.

How much he'd missed her.

How much he'd missed out on.

The longing was sharp, a painful jab to his heart.

God, she was pretty and sweet and had once loved him like

no one else had ever done so. Leaving her had been the hardest thing he'd ever done, trailed a close second by staying away, by not contacting her to beg her for forgiveness. He'd kept discreet tabs on her, just to make sure she was safe, and those reports from his security combined with the risk he presented to her were what gave him the strength to not come back.

Until now.

Until the papers had been delivered, demanding he excise himself from the final hold he had on her life.

He couldn't cut that tie.

And now that he'd seen her again, seen what she built . . . *fuck*, he was so incredibly proud of her, proud of what she'd built. Without him. On her own. She'd always been smart and capable, but she'd lacked confidence. Jackson hadn't minded that, which probably made him an asshole.

But the woman in front of him wasn't just sweet and warm. She was comfortable in her skin, filling the space with an air of competence.

This Molly was different than the woman he'd almost married.

She was more.

Because he'd left.

Which then bore the question of whether or not he should just leave again. If he came back, would he ruin that?

He watched her check the case then disappear back through the door. His cell buzzed again, but he still didn't glance at it. She would come back and then—

She emerged with a large tray held in both arms, efficiently filling the rows of the case with a variety of pastries and sandwiches. After, she flipped a screen and turned the menu to reveal the lunch offerings then smiled at the petite brunette behind the counter who nodded, smiled back, and disappeared into the kitchen.

Jackson studied Molly's even motions, the way she moved. He knew she did it without thinking—wiping down the countertops, the register, scanning then restocking napkins and silverware on the unit that held the supplies, before making a sweep of the dining room with a gray plastic tub and collecting leftover mugs and plates then cleaning off the tables and picking up small plastic placards with numbers on them. In less than ten minutes the space was clean and ready for lunch.

Well, everywhere except where he sat.

The employee had come over to gather up Ronnie's plate and mug earlier, but she hadn't wiped down the pale white wood with him sitting there, and Molly had certainly given his table a wide berth before returning back behind the counter.

His phone buzzed again, and he glanced down, saw it was his assistant. Again. The office was probably freaking out. He didn't take days off, let alone disappear without his computer. Frankly, he was scared to think of what his inbox would look like when he got back to his office, the minimal replies he'd done via his cell akin to trying to put out a forest fire with an eye dropper.

The final patrons got up from the last occupied table and left. They disappeared out the front door, the quiet tinkling of the bell cheerful. And that was the only bit of cheerful in the whole space because when Jackson glanced toward the register, the look Molly gave him was chilly.

Probably, wondering why he didn't just sign the papers and follow them out.

He should.

He wasn't going to.

He'd done a lot of things wrong when it came to Molly and if he was going to fix that, then he needed to level with her.

Well, first, it would be good if he were able to get her to listen to him.

At least long enough to level with her, because if she didn't understand why he'd done what he'd done, if she didn't forgive him then he . . .

Would leave?

Everything inside him had stilled.

He'd done that. He'd buried himself in work, he'd eschewed his family, women, friends. He'd left everything behind.

And what had that gotten him?

Absolutely fucking nothing.

Well, he was done with nothing.

The papers arriving on his desk were a timely reminder that this was his chance to make things right. If Molly didn't want to listen to him, to forgive him, well, he wasn't leaving. He'd make her understand, make her realize he'd *had* to do what he'd done.

Make her understand that he hadn't wanted to, but that things had gotten complicated and . . .

He needed to make her see that things would be different now.

He *would* make her see that.

Decided, he stood, detouring to the table when the phone rang, picking up the plates and mugs, depositing them into the gray bin she'd carried around, grabbing the towel and spray she'd used to wipe the table, and giving everything a good clean.

He couldn't remember the last time he'd so much as cleaned up after himself. His dirty dishes were efficiently swept away, his toilet and sink scrubbed, his clothes picked up from the floor and laundered, his food prepared and placed in front of him fresh and hot no matter the hour he stumbled in from his office.

Coddled.

Surrounded by people.

And yet, alone.

Molly had never made him feel alone. She'd seen him as a

person, not a meal ticket, as someone to love rather than a commodity, as—

She'd loved him, and he'd had to shit on that love to make sure she stayed alive.

Now, he would do anything to have that love back.

He *was* going to do anything to get it back.

FIVE

Molly

SHE SAW Jackson get up and took advantage of the phone ringing to turn her back on him, relief pouring through her when the bell tinkled, signaling his exit.

Thank God.

He was a stubborn man, but she'd gone toe-to-toe with him plenty. He knew he couldn't out-stubborn her.

He'd sign the papers. Be done. Leave like he was so fucking good at.

Good riddance.

And no, that wasn't a fucking slice of disappointment she felt as she hung up the phone and carefully made a few final notes on the large catering order.

She'd been done with Jackson four years ago. She was still finished with him—

"I can't wait to get my tongue on your sweet treat."

Velvet. Rasp. Honey down her spine. A heatwave between her thighs. Molly spun and saw that she was wrong. Jackson hadn't left. He stood just feet away, leaning against the counter, one ankle crossed over the other and looking altogether too sexy for her own good. Tall and lean with narrow hips and defined arms, he was more swimmer than bodybuilder. But that was fine. That was her preference, her type.

Jackson Davis was her kryptonite.

But she wasn't a weakling, wasn't susceptible to a line that should have been sleazy and creepy, and instead threatened to melt her from the inside out. She had spine—spine that had become lined with steel over the last few years. Steel she took advantage of in that moment. "You're a fucking pig," she snapped.

He grinned.

Her stomach went a little more melty.

No, she wasn't proud of it. But thus was the power of Jackson. Her pussy knew exactly what he could do for it and was critically aware that it had been four years since her last orgasm of the Davis variety.

And those orgasms were special. He didn't need a road map to find her clit, his tongue was fucking magical, and . . . he knew her body almost better than she did.

Pathetic?

Probably.

Had she reaped the benefits during their time together?

Hell-fucking-yes, she had.

And there he stood, still grinning, not upset at her snapping, not pissed that she'd called him a pig. But then again, he'd always reacted that way. Provoking her then seeming to gobble up her anger, as though he craved her fury.

Her nipples perked up at the memory.

Pathetic round two.

She sighed. "Why are you here?" she asked, dropping her hands to the counter and letting her head fall forward as she rolled out her shoulders.

Silence.

Molly glanced up after a long moment, saw that he'd moved, but just as she processed that Jackson wasn't in front of her, that he might have gone, she sensed him behind her. His spicy scent surrounded her, and she started to spin.

But he caught her shoulders, stopped her motion. "I got you, honey."

Then those hands slid up slightly and began massaging the tight muscles there. She knew she should stop him, knew that with every brain cell she possessed, but the second he touched her, all common sense faded.

Because it felt good to have him touch her.

And seriously, how fucked up was she that it felt good to have this man touch her?

He knew exactly where her muscles ached, how the pain radiated into her neck, down her right arm. He remembered how hard to press so the knots went away, but not so hard as to hurt her.

He. Remembered.

Her spine softened, body instinctively arching to brush her ass against his pelvis, hearing his breath hiss out.

She got wet.

Just that easily.

But it was always like that with him. One touch and she was hot for him. One touch and she was hot enough to almost make her forget that she hated this man who had his hands on her.

"I didn't want to leave you," he murmured into her ear.

Cold washed over her, that heat gone in an instant. She spun, knocked his hands away. "Don't fucking touch me," she hissed. "Don't you *fucking* touch—"

"Baby—"

"No," she said, ice in her veins. "You don't get to call me

that. You don't get to put your hands on me. Not when you left like you did. Not when you—"

"Molly—"

"Leave me the fuck alone, Jackson." She shoved him back a step. "Just leave. You're really fucking good at that." Another shove, pushing him clear of the counter. "I don't need you in my life." One more and he was out from behind it, back on the customer side. "I don't need you here. I don't want—"

"They were going to kill you."

Her hands, raised and ready for another push, dropped to her sides. Her jaw fell open. Of all the excuses she could have imagined him to come up with, that was right up there with the last thing she would have expected him to say.

He hesitated then took a step closer, moving behind the counter again, and his voice dropping. "I got mixed up in a bad deal with some bad people. I realized it, but I was in deep." Another step. "Baby, I thought I could handle it, could get myself, my business out without any consequences . . . but then they involved you."

Molly froze.

"You," he whispered, taking another step toward her, until they were almost touching. "I couldn't let them involve you."

"H-how—" She cleared her throat. "How did they—?"

An expression crossed his face, one that she now realized she'd seen a lot during those final months they been together. Warring. He was warring with himself. But then he pulled out his cell, tapped on the screen a few times then held it out to her.

She'd just reached to take it when the bell above the door dinged.

They both whirled, saw that a group of women were bustling in. They were regulars, had been coming in since not long after she'd opened. Seeing Jackson behind the counter, they froze and Abby, a brunette with a baby on her hip, asked, "Are you okay, Molly?"

She forced herself to smile. "I'm good. You guys go ahead and take your normal table. Jeanine will come out to get your drinks." Then she took Jackson's hand and tugged him through the swinging door, finding her employee washing her hands.

"I'm just finishing . . ." Jeanine trailed off, no doubt stunned by the Tall, Dark, and Handsome suddenly appearing in the kitchen.

Another forced smile. "This is Jackson. We'll be in my office. Can you cover Abby and company? Michelle will be in for the lunch rush in just a few minutes."

Mutely, Jeanine nodded. But didn't move.

"They're at their usual table," Molly prompted.

Jeanine blinked, eyes flying from over Molly's head—and probably from Jackson's face—down to Molly's. "Got it," Jeanine said, and with another long, lingering look above Molly's head, disappeared through the door leading to the front of house.

"You do table service now?" Jackson asked.

She tugged his hand again, leading him toward her office. "Just for a few regulars."

Silence.

Her eyes slanted up to his, but she couldn't read the emotion there. "What?"

"You have regulars now."

Yeah, she did.

"Fuck, honey, you did it."

Her lungs seized. Just straight up froze in her chest, stopped moving, stopped functioning . . . because he was proud. She could hear it so damned clearly in his tone.

A shake of her head.

It didn't matter if he were proud of her. He'd left—

But maybe he hadn't wanted to go—?

Didn't matter.

But maybe it did. Hell . . . she didn't know anything except that she had to finish this discussion, that spending five minutes with Jackson might give her clarity and let her finally move on with her life. She was tired of just living for the bakery. She wanted more. But when Jackson had left, she'd built a wall around herself, an impenetrable barrier between her inner self and the superficial. She could charm an unhappy patron in a flash, had created a happy and relaxed work environment for her employees, but she hadn't opened herself up to the world. It was all fluff while keeping her vulnerable center safe.

She hadn't realized that she'd reached her office, that she'd stopped outside the door until Jackson's front came very close to her back, hand lifting to turn the handle and push open the door.

Heat on her spine.

Spice in her nose.

Longing between her thighs.

Blinking, she forced her feet to move, to enter her office, to cross around her desk and put some space between them, to give her a few seconds to clamp down on the effect his body had on hers.

She was a businesswoman. She had spine. She wasn't a weakling when it came to her desires.

But *how* she wanted to be.

Tamping down the urge and lifting her chin, she settled into her office chair, waving an imperious hand at the wooden one in front of her desk.

Jackson's lips twitched.

Then he ignored her wave, ignored the chair, and rounded her desk, propping his hip on it. "Molly," he murmured.

And she realized she'd made a critical error. Now, he was

between her and the exit. Now he was close, and she *wanted*.
Now . . . he held out his cell again.

She saw what was on the screen and the longing
disappeared.

She saw the image and the bottom fell out of the world she
thought she knew.

She saw the image, and so many pieces fell into place.

SIX

Jackson

HE REALIZED about two heartbeats after Molly saw what was on the screen that he'd bungled this.

Words would have been better than the image that had been the final straw.

The photograph had convinced him to leave her.

It was of Molly, taken in her kitchen four years before. The construction on the bakery had just been completed, and everything was new and shiny. But that wasn't the part that had made him pull the plug on their relationship. No, the reason he'd finally capitulated to the threats he'd been receiving with ever-increasing frequency was because of the red dot centered on her forehead, and the angle of the photograph.

They'd been in her shop.

They'd had a gun trained on her.

And his Molly had been wearing her headphones, her gaze on the dough on the table in front of her as she carefully deposited perfect slices of apples. She'd had a smile on her face, completely oblivious to the fact that a bullet could have torn through her skull.

A smile on her face when a gun had been pointed at her head.

He'd received that image the morning of the wedding.

And that was the moment he'd stopped trying to handle things on his own. That was the moment he called in the best, most expensive security he could afford for Molly. That was the moment he'd contacted the authorities.

And *that* was the moment he'd known he had to cut Molly loose.

In a way that was public.

In a way that made it absolutely clear he no longer had feelings for her.

In a way that made it certain she'd keep her distance, that she wouldn't bring herself back into the crosshairs of the. Fucking. Russian. Mafia.

Who knew that finding a long-awaited investor for his software company would be his undoing?

Fuck. He'd been so thrilled to finally have been able to roll out his new product.

He just didn't realize that doing so would put the woman he loved at risk from a corrupt foreign power who had no compunction about killing anyone in order to get their way.

"Wh-what is this?"

"It's why I left, Mol."

Pale green eyes on his. "I-I don't understand."

"I fucked up, sweetheart," he said. "I accepted some money from people I shouldn't have then dismissed the threats until they made it clear that I *couldn't* dismiss them." With that photo.

She dropped the cell to her desk, pushed up from her chair,

and paced away from him. Five steps from him she stopped, spun around. "When?"

"What?"

"When did you find this out?"

His brows drew down. "They sent the picture the morning of the wedding."

Her eyes slid closed then opened slowly, understanding in their peridot depths. "That's why you didn't show."

"I couldn't."

"This wasn't the first threat."

Her words weren't a question, but rather a statement, and he knew he owed her nothing less than the absolute truth. "No."

"Ah." Molly tilted her head back and was so still that she could have been a statue. But then she released a long, shaking breath. "And is there a reason that you didn't tell me that any of this was going on?"

The question was deceptively calm.

"I—"

It was probably just as well that she only let him get that one syllable out. Because he *didn't* have a good reason, other than the fact that he'd thought he was doing the right thing by protecting her.

"Your life was threatened. *My* life was threatened," she said, pushing past him and pacing again. "And you thought what? That I couldn't handle knowing? That I was too weak to know the truth?" She turned, closed the distance between them, and jabbed a finger into his chest. "I was going to be your wife. We were supposed to be partners, and the fact that our lives were at risk didn't register even a mention on your list of things you should talk to me about?"

She had a valid point. One he hadn't quite grasped until that exact moment.

"Baby—"

"Molly," she corrected.

"Molly," he said. "You're right." He reached for her hand, but she stepped back, not allowing the contact. "*Of course*, you're right. I wasn't thinking clearly about any of it. Everything got so big and out of control so quickly, and . . . I didn't know what to do."

"No."

He blinked. "No?"

She shook her head. "No, Jackson. You didn't keep this from me because you were scared or were trying to protect me. Or not *only* for those reasons," she added when he opened his mouth to reply. "You didn't think I could handle it."

He froze, started to tell her that, no, he hadn't thought that. Except . . .

This Molly, the one standing in front of him, the one who was so capably running a business, who was taking this news without hysteria and tears, without fury, was a very different Molly from the one he'd been engaged to. *That* Molly had been a little fragile, already under stress from the wedding and the new business. That Molly had loved him with a depth he'd never doubted . . . and if he was admitting it, he'd liked that devotion.

It had fed his ego to have someone so utterly committed to him. He'd *liked* that she'd almost been more involved in his life than her own, that she knew what clients he was meeting with every day, that she sent deliveries to his office tailored to what they preferred. He liked that she'd made dinner every night, that she had picked up his dry cleaning, that he'd never once had to make a run for food or stop at the grocery store on the way home from work.

Fuck. He was an even bigger asshole than he'd thought.

She sighed, dropped into her chair, leaning her head back and closing her eyes. "Anything else?"

"What?" His gut was churning from what he'd just realized, guilt swelling within him, a wave that had begun when he'd received the papers, one that had continued to gain height as he'd debated coming to the bakery, then had grown bigger as he'd seen what she'd built. One that was pounding into him, trapping him against the rocks that lined the shore as it beat against him again and again and *again*. He'd hurt her without realizing it, hadn't appreciated her, had taken and taken and would have *continued* to take if he hadn't broken things off.

He would have sucked her dry until she was nothing more than a shell of herself.

And that made him fucking despicable.

"Is there anything else you kept from me?" she asked, eyes still closed.

Throat tight, he said, "No." It was the truth. There was nothing except for the fact that the photograph had shown him how much of a close call she'd dodged when he'd called off the wedding.

Molly sighed again, eyes opening, those pretty green eyes locking with his. "I hated you for what you did. For a long time, I absolutely hated you." She pushed up from her chair. "But honestly? You did me a favor, Jackson. I wasn't . . . fully formed four years ago. I was living off you, making my whole life yours. I was *weak*." One step and she was close enough that her scent surrounded him.

Sweet. Fuck, she always smelled so damned sweet.

But also . . . in that moment, he'd never felt more sure that she was too fucking good for him.

Another step, her moving past him toward the door again.

He'd spent the day getting his fill. He'd leveled with her. He'd made it clear it wasn't her fault.

Should he have done that four years ago? Fucking, *of course*, he should have.

Could he build a time machine and go back, fix what he'd done? No.

But could he make it better for her now, take a worry off her shoulders, remove himself from her life, one he had no right interfering in? Yes.

Jackson heard the *click* just as he opened his mouth to announce that he was going to sign the papers and remove himself once and for all. He frowned and spun toward the sound.

"You hurt me."

Then, suddenly, Molly was there, within arm's reach, looking so fucking beautiful that he couldn't imagine how he could have ever left her.

But he'd been a different man then.

"I know I did," he said. "And I'm sorry. I was wrong . . . about so many things."

Her expression hardened. She took another step toward him. "Yes."

"If I could change it, if I could go back and—"

She rose on tiptoe, eyes coming level with his, hurt swimming in their depths. "You can't go back." A beat. "*We* can't go back, Jackson."

"I—"

Molly kissed him.

SEVEN

Molly

SHE WAS PROBABLY AN IDIOT.

Hell, she was *definitely* an idiot.

But he'd shown her that photograph, she'd seen the dot on her forehead, and terror had gripped her for long enough that her lungs had frozen and she'd felt her mind swim from a lack of oxygen.

It was a violation, and just because it was a violation from four years ago didn't mean she couldn't understand.

Jackson hadn't been thinking.

He hadn't broken it off because of her.

And . . . she'd felt no little amount of relief.

Not her. Not her. Not—

He'd gone still when her lips had touched his, rigid like a metal statue, his hands at his sides, their bodies not touching except for their mouths. But now he unfroze and exploded into a flurry of motion that sent all thoughts of idiocy and relief and *not her* from her mind.

Because this was Jackson, and this was her . . . and *this* had never been their problem.

His hands came up, one clamping onto her hip, the other sliding up her spine to weave into the messy ponytail at the base of her neck that was containing her riotous brown curls. A second later that elastic disappeared, and his fingers were combing through her hair, the pads resting against her scalp.

God, she'd missed that, missed him cradling her against him, angling her head just slightly so their lips were perfectly aligned. Missed how just the touch of his mouth against hers somehow righted everything in the universe.

Then his tongue brushed against the seam of her lips.

She didn't think, didn't hesitate, just parted and let him in. Their tongues tangled and stroked. He tugged her more firmly against his body and then they kissed and kissed and *kissed*. Eventually, though, he started to slow the flurried movements of his tongue, began to loosen the grip on her hip, ease his hand from her hair.

No.

She didn't want him to stop, to slow, to pull back.

She leaned in, throwing her arms around his neck, plastering herself against his chest.

He tore his lips away. "Mol—"

"Kiss me, Jackson. Make me forget."

A long moment of hesitation, his deep chocolate eyes locked onto hers, but then she tilted her pelvis, brushed against the hard length of his erection, and he groaned, banded his arms more tightly around her then dropped his head.

Lips on lips.

Hard against soft.

Duel moans. Hers because this was as right as she'd felt in the last four years. His because . . . well, she hoped he felt an inkling of the same.

But Molly didn't stop to process or think. She weaved her hands into *his* hair, climbed up his body, wrapped her legs around his waist, and kissed him. She nipped at his bottom lip, tilted *his* head, swept her tongue deep to taste the spiced heat of his mouth.

The flavor of the cinnamon gum he preferred.

The bitter tang of the coffee he must have drank that morning.

The faintest hint of mint from his toothpaste.

Ambrosia.

Jackson.

Right.

He straightened from the desk, lifting her into his arms and spun, shooting an arm out, sending her keyboard clattering to the floor, dumping the cup of pencils, the small wooden cylinders hitting the tile with a series of rapid *tap tap taps*. The next second she was on her back, splayed out like she was a plate of chocolate cookies placed in the center of a group of very hungry, PMS-ing women.

Hot eyes, reddened lips. An erection outlined by the thin material of his slacks.

She wanted him, wanted him to make her feel like she used to, wanted to forget everything that had happened.

For one moment, she just wanted to feel good.

"Mol—"

"Fuck me, Jackson," she said, heart pounding, breaths coming in short bursts. Her need was on a razor's point, almost painful. This close to him, so long since she'd felt anything as remotely strong as the pull they had when they were together. "I need you to just fuck me."

His fingers tightened on her hips, jaw tightening. "That's not—"

"Help me," she moaned. "Help me forget." She wrapped her legs around his waist, drawing him close.

He groaned, thrust against her then stopped, head hanging, breath in rapid gusts. "Baby, we—"

"Please." She reached for him. "Please, Jackson."

Only the briefest hesitation before he bent, lips pausing a hairsbreadth from hers. "Okay, baby." He brushed her mouth. "I got you."

He reached for the button of her jeans, flicked it open, and slid his hand inside.

"Oh fuck," she moaned. T   :oughened palm sliding under her underwear, fingers   through her wet pussy was the best ever.

Well, until his thumb circ   it and pressed.

Hard.

She arched off the desl   beaded and aching, moisture pooling between her th   :h kept trying to spread but were hindered by the st   ial of the denim. Jackson slipped his hand free, and   ə a noise in protest, but just as the sound passed her lips, he reared back and yanked off her sneakers.

They hit the floor one after another, were followed by her jeans, by her underwear.

And then Jackson was on his knees, shouldering her thighs apart, mouth descending . . .

"Fuuuck," she breathed, head clonking back against the desk.

No one could tongue fuck her like Jackson could.

He slid his tongue through her labia, stopping to suck at one spot on the right side that never failed to make her squirm and groan, to ratchet her arousal to epic proportions before continuing up, kissing and licking . . . and sucking her clit like it was a hard candy he was determined to finish before the principal caught him with the sweet treat between his lips.

I can't wait to get my tongue on your sweet treat.

What should have been the cheesiest, worst line in the history of all lines, sent heat skittering down her spine for a second time.

He had his tongue on her and when he murmured, "So fucking sweet," against her pussy, Molly imploded.

Just that easily.

Because with Jackson, it had always been heat and speed, ease and comfort, allowing herself to be swallowed by the wave of his presence.

Pleasure exploded from her center, flying through her limbs, pulsing outward, filling her with fire. She moaned loudly and found his hand covering her lips to stifle the sound, even as his tongue coaxed her through to the other side, gently caressed her down from the precipice.

That wave covered her, comforted, even as it sucked her under.

It was only when he reached for her panties and started to tug them over her feet that she realized what he was about.

Stopping.

"Jackson," she said.

"I'm going, baby."

Was he fucking kidding? He was going to blow back into her life, eat her out like it was his fucking job, and then leave her wanting him?

No.

Not this time.

She was driving this.

And she wanted the man's cock inside her.

Maybe it was selfish. Maybe it was using him. Maybe she

was pissed and hurting and overwhelmed and this was the stupidest thing she could do.

But fuck it all.

She'd spent too long being unselfish with this man.

For once, she could reach for what *she* wanted.

For once, that could be okay.

Molly moved, kicking off the underwear, pushing off the desk, and grabbing the front of Jackson's button-down. She yanked him against her and rose up to slant her lips across his.

He kissed her back and it was all teeth and tongue, nipping and stroking, sparking her sated desire back into an inferno. He grabbed her hips, pulling her s   ainst him, grinding the hardness of his cock against h

She reached down, open   .ton of his slacks, yanking at the zipper, fighting with t   .il until . . . *finally*.

His cock was hard and   , her hand.

Molly shoved at his   ng them past his hips before lifting a leg and wrappi   id his waist, angling him until he was positioned just

"Baby—"

She tilted her pelvis and ok him inside.

Fuck. Yes.

They both hissed out a breath as he stretched her wide, the burn of him amping up her pleasure. It had been so long, and this felt so fucking right.

She jumped slightly, wrapped the other leg around him, taking him deeper.

"Fuck me, honey," she moaned, arching back, feeling him bottom out, a harsh guttural curse vibrating through her.

Then there were no more words. No delays or hesitations.

His hands came to her ass, and he spun them, pinned her between the wall and his chest.

And then he moved.

He pounded into her, a little hard, a little rough, not smooth and sweet and gentle in the least. It was fast and intense . . . and it was the best fucking ever.

Literally.

The. Best. *Fucking*. Ever.

The hard circles of his shirt buttons were digging into her chest, the strap of her apron was abrading the skin of her neck, his zipper scratched her thighs . . . and those little pains didn't take anything away. In fact, they heightened the experience, elevated it. He kept thrusting, hard and thick and hot, his scorching breath puffing against her skin, his groans vibrating through her.

"Fuck, baby," he gritted out. "Baby, tell me you're there with me."

"Almost," she panted. "I need—"

He knew what she needed even before she finished the sentence. He altered the angle of his thrusts, so that each time he bottomed out, he rubbed against her clit, and then he shifted one hand, fingers sliding along the crease of her ass, moving in, pressing against her with his thumb until he was fucking both of her holes, finger and cock moving in unison.

"I'm—" She broke off. "Jackson— *Fuck!*"

She was there, her orgasm exploding through her.

He ground into her once, twice, a third time and groaned, holding deep, his cock pulsing as he came inside her.

They stayed like that for a long time, Jackson still hard and planted deep, their breathing rapid and staccato, their skin sticky with sweat.

But the longer they stayed like that, the harder it was to keep her mind focused on just feeling. Memories kept creeping to the forefront of her mind. How she'd felt when he hadn't shown up at the church. The panic of searching the hospitals. How broken she'd been after the scene in the police station.

Her breathing had been slowing, but now it started to speed up again, horror washing through her.

This was either her getting swept along with the tsunami that was Jackson or it was her taking advantage of a man's guilt just so she could have a couple of orgasms. "You—"

Jackson moved without her finishing the sentence, slipping out, steadying her as she found her feet.

Then her panties.

She slid them up her th   'e a grab for her jeans and yanked them up her legs.

"We shouldn't have dor

He'd stolen her words,   it *she* should have said.

"You're right," she agr   dded, "You should go."

At the very least, she   that.

Because if she told F   then she wouldn't ask him to stay.

Jackson's eyes drift∈   ving to lock with hers, holding for a long, drawn-out m   it he didn't ask to stay either.

He just finished doing up his pants, straightened the cuffs of his shirt, and headed for the door, pausing with his hand on the knob. "For what it's worth, I know that I did the wrong thing, and I'm sorry for that." He turned the handle, opened the door. "But I'm not sorry it kept you safe."

He stepped out into the hall, closed the wooden panel behind him.

"Not sorry," she muttered, doing up her own pants, smoothing her apron. "That sounds about right."

But she didn't mean the words.

Of course, she didn't.

And anyway, she was too wrapped up in the conflicting thoughts in her mind to really mean anything.

Was she the user or the usee?

So, instead of thinking about it further or the fact that she'd had to go to the bathroom to put in a tampon, rather than spending the remainder of the day with the reminder of Jackson dripping out from between her thighs, she took care of the problem, washed her hands, and deliberately ignored the random pulses of pleasure that continued to crop up as the hours passed.

Instead, in what was probably a sick circle of events, she spent the rest of the day making apple turnovers, the same ones she'd been making in the photograph that had torn them apart.

Only this time, there wasn't anyone around.

Or at least there wasn't anyone around who had the urge to shine a bright red laser on her forehead.

Molly was wrong about the last.

She just didn't find out how wrong until much later.

THE NEXT DAY she woke up early, got dressed, and stumbled through her morning, the early hours feeling all that much earlier because she'd hardly slept the night before.

Jackson Davis.

Not the bad guy she'd made him out to be.

Especially when, shortly after five in the morning, as Molly was finishing up loading the case in the front of the bakery, the bell chimed over the door and a young male in an expensive suit strode inside.

"Molly Miller?" he asked, approaching the counter.

"Yes?" she replied, confusion drawing her brows together.

"These are for you from Mr. Davis." He extended a manila envelope in her direction.

"What—?" she began to ask.

But by then she'd opened the flap and recognized what was inside.

The papers she'd had couriered to Jackson—signed,

although with an addendum saying she'd bought Jackson out for a dollar instead of the fair market price she'd offered previously.

Signed.

Done.

Out of her life.

Perfect. That was exactly what she wanted.

And if she thought that perhaps, deep down, she might not *actually* want Jackson out of her life for good, if it were the sliver of a thought, the barest thread of a wish, Molly was great at pretending she didn't see or feel it.

She was excellent at pretending.

She'd made it her life's work.

EIGHT

Jackson, A month later

HE STRODE out of his office after nine at night and bit back a curse when he saw the man waiting in the reception area.

"Dan," he said, shoving his cell into his pocket and coming to a stop. "Do you take some pleasure in sneaking into my office?"

This late at night, the building was locked down, the floor to his office doubly so.

Dan shrugged. "Gotta keep your security on their toes."

At the mention of security, one of Jackson's expensive as hell security team members appeared in the hall, his body tensed and readied as though he were heading into battle. Jackson caught the man's gaze and shook his head. "We're fine."

Dan waited until the guard left, who backed slowly down the hall with a glare at the sneaky agent, before he turned to Jackson and gestured the opposite direction.

Jackson took the hint, led the way to the corner office that had become his home away from home. His company had recently taken over the top five floors of this building, retrofitting and modifying the space, and moving in just a few weeks before.

All at prime San Franciscan prices.

The location was more about the perception of power rather than actual power, but Jackson *had* managed to secure some truly reliable—and not criminal—investors in the last few years, ones that didn't want to use his product to conduct corporate espionage or to unleash an army of bots to try and divide the American people online.

He'd gotten better at discerning, and his business had grown.

But old problems persisted.

Case in point, the man in front of him.

"It's good to see you, Davis."

"I wish I could say the same, Plantain," he muttered, because apparently they were switching to last names. He strode through the door to his office, leaned back against his desk and tried to ignore the memory of doing the same on Molly's desk . . . and what had happened after. "What are you doing here? Pretending to be in town to watch your sister play again?"

Dan's sister was a goalie for the San Francisco Gold, the newest expansion team in the NHL.

But hockey didn't run in the family.

Dan was part of a nameless government agency, a member of a team that had shown up about eight hours after Jackson had called the FBI to report the threats and the dirty investors in his company.

He was also part of the team that was supposed to have already taken down the investor and dismantled the criminal organization, a clan of the Russian mob called the Mikhailova, that had provided it.

"You're clearly not a sports man," Dan said. "It's not even hockey season."

Jackson sighed, didn't take the bait. Truth was, he *wasn't* much of a sports man. He was too busy saving the business he'd almost torpedoed and then doing his limited part to root out the bad guys involved. "Why are you here?"

Dan sprawled into one of the chairs and announced, "We've had a setback."

Fury tore through him. "This shit was supposed to have been done two fucking years ago."

No sympathy on the agent's face. "Sorry to be the one to tell you this, but life doesn't always work out the way you want it."

Jackson cursed and thrust a hand through his hair. He knew that. He'd lived that life for the last four years, had tried to stop himself from having to live it for the previous year before that. All for nothing. In the end, he'd had to give everything important up anyway.

Molly gone.

His business in tatters.

"You are *not* going to tell me to make lemonade out of lemons."

"How about lemon cake?" Dan said, still sprawling though he smacked his lips. "Fuck, I love lemon cake. In fact, I could go for—"

"What's the setback?" Jackson said, interrupting him before he could go full soliloquy on the merits of lemon cake. Having heard more than a few of Dan's tangents over the years, he knew they were neither short nor particularly meaningful.

"You."

Jackson frowned. "What the fuck are you talking about?"

"You shouldn't have gone to see her, man," Dan said, and that one sentence twisted Jackson's stomach into knots.

He pushed up from the desk and got in Dan's face. Probably not the smartest thing, especially when he could see the outline of a weapon on the other man's hip. But fury had overshadowed common sense, at least for the moment "What. The. Fuck. Are you talking about?"

"They saw you go to her."

Jackson's heart seized and his throat constricted. "It's been four years."

"They saw."

"It was only a couple of hours." Hours riddled with both pleasure and guilt.

"Time doesn't matter with these guys."

"Fuck." He leaned back, paced the length of his office. "*Fuck!*" He turned back. "What are we going to do?"

"I've got protection on her."

Jackson snorted. "The same protection that resulted in her having a fucking gun pointed at her head?"

Dan sighed. "My advice is to continue staying away. Leave her to her life, make sure these guys know that she doesn't mean anything to you, make sure they don't use her to get to you. Leave her alone so she can be safe."

"I did that already, and it didn't work."

"You went back."

"I—" Jackson cut off his excuse. He'd been about to say he'd had to talk to her about the papers, but that was a lie. He could have signed and been done without seeing her. He could have left when she'd so clearly wanted him to. He could have not fucked her against the wall in the single best sexual experience of his life before finally abiding by her wishes and leaving. He'd ruined so much, taken so much—

"Just stay away."

How could he? He'd tried that for four years. Then one morning in her presence, and he was right back where he'd begun. Obsessing about Molly, thinking of her every waking moment, fighting with himself to not go back to the bakery, to not beg and plead and make her understand that his life without her was meaningless.

Maybe if he hadn't seen her, he could have continued to resist. Maybe the urge to go back wouldn't be so acute.

But he *had* gone back.

And now Jackson was in agony.

"You can't stay away, can you?" Dan asked quietly.

Silence.

Then, "No."

"Fuck." Dan pulled out his cell, considered for a few seconds then began typing. Within a half-minute of him hitting the final key and placing it on his thigh, there was a buzz, signaling a response. He nodded. "If I told you to give me three more months, could you do it?"

Jackson stifled a curse. *No*, he couldn't do it. But could he also risk Molly just because he might be in agony for another ninety days?

Also, no.

"Fuck, no, you can't," Dan muttered, typing on his cell again. "Okay, here's what we're going to do. *This* is no longer your office. Your office is the bakery. Your ass is in a chair at Molly's place anytime she's there. Your presence is known and expected and constant."

Jackson frowned.

"It's not a deterrent so much as a declaration. Molly is yours. If you're always there, they'll see she belongs with you. That they have to fuck with you to get to her."

More frowning. "They've made it pretty clear they don't mind fucking with me. Isn't this going to just unleash more shit onto her?"

"The shit's already coming, Jackson. But we can just use this to our advantage. Push them to make a move sooner than they're ready." Dan shoved his phone in his pocket. "It's not foolproof. It's dangerous. But the *whole* situation is dangerous. So, if you really can't give me a few months then you have to be prepared to be all in."

"I've *been* in. *Fuck*, Dan. I've done everything you've asked of me. I left the woman I loved. I stayed away from her for years." He paced away again. "I gave you access to my company, to every document and email and bank account. I did *everything—*"

"And you've got nothing to show for it," Dan said quietly. "I know, brother. I know what that's like."

"Fuck," he hissed, knowing that he had to make a decision.

Knowing the decision was already made.

Molly.

It was all for Molly.

He sucked in a breath, released it slowly. "Tell me exactly what I need to do."

NINE

Molly

ZERO-DARK THIRTY.

Stumbling out of bed.

Attempting to corral her hair, to pull on clothes that coordinated—sort of—shoes that matched—occasionally proving more difficult, especially when comparing black to navy.

Today, she settled with plain gray sneakers with jeans and a T-shirt that was emblazoned with the bakery's logo.

Easy. Simple.

Necessary.

She hadn't slept well since the day a month before when Jackson had walked back into her life, her dreams punctured by memories of him, by memories of *after* him.

Which made getting up at three-thirty in the morning seriously unforgiving.

Thankfully, she'd managed to hire a second baker, so her early mornings were now limited to the three middle days during the week—Tuesday, Wednesday, and Thursday.

Being able to sleep until six on the other days made it so she could function.

She may not be thriving, but at least she could function.

And she knew that was a win.

Head down, move forward, keep going, and things would be okay, wounds would heal, shattered hearts would be pieced back together, a spine would be strengthened and able to hold a head high.

Her coffee pot was already percolating, that first mug filled, her travel carafe next to it, readied for its own supply.

Molly made the switch, set the maker to go another time and it began rumbling, popping, and hissing as it filled the To-Go cup that was the second necessary piece of her wake-up routine.

The first being that initial mug ready to go.

She picked it up, blew on the hot liquid, then drank quickly, ignoring the burn of the too-hot coffee, relishing the spike as the caffeine hit her system, shaking the clouds from her mind and enabling her to locate her purse, keys, and cell.

By the time the travel carafe was full, her mug was empty, and she was awake enough to operate a motor vehicle.

She set the empty mug in the sink, grabbed her stuff—and the To-Go coffee—then headed out the front door of her duplex.

And almost mowed down a man.

The scream caught in her throat, then dissipated when she saw it was Jackson, her mouth dropping open.

What. The. Fuck?

Before she could unstick enough to verbalize that thought, he stepped close, *real* close, and brushed his mouth across her cheek, very near her ear, in which he whispered, "I'll explain in the car." Then he swept her purse from her hands, wrapped an arm around her waist and started leading her to a vehicle that was not hers.

She repeated. What. The. Fuck?

But when her feet started to skitter, to fight the forward motion, Jackson bent again and nipped her ear. "Don't fight me. It's not safe. Car, baby." Her eyes flew up, saw that his jaw was tight, his body stiff, even though his voice had been gentle . . . and so it seemed smarter in that moment to *not* argue, to just walk to his car.

To allow him to open the door and help her inside.

To wait until he'd started the engine and then pulled out of the spot to burst out with, "What the fuck, Jackson Davis?"

His gaze cut to hers then returned to the road, navigating the nearly empty streets with all the care of a professional driver navigating the world's most important race.

"I'm here," he stated calmly.

That was it. *I'm here.*

As though that were supposed to bring some clarity to the situation when he'd disappeared and come back then disappeared again—

You asked him to go.

Yeah, there was that.

So, she stifled the temper that only seemed to ramp when Jackson was around and forced herself to calmly ask, "Why are you here?"

Silence for an interminable stretch.

Then, "It goes against every grain in me to tell you this, when I feel like I should be protecting you, not telling you something that will make you terrified," he said, and just that precursor to the explanation was terrifying. Add in the careful tone, the stiffness in his jaw, his body, and the hairs on the back of her neck rose. "But I promised myself that I wouldn't carry anymore secrets. You deserve to know the truth of what's happening."

Molly swallowed hard then asked, "And what's the truth?"

"The truth is that when I came to the bakery a month ago, I brought you back into the focus of the Russian mafia."

Oh, fuck.

"When I came, when I stayed, they realized you still had value to me, and they'll exploit that connection to get what they want."

Double fuck.

"The government knows, they've been following you and protecting you since they found out from their source that you're back in the crosshairs, but they're also close to shutting this cell down, close to giving the group a death blow that will put them out of commission for many years, if not forever."

That was great. Eliminating the mafia forever sounded like a good thing.

Yet Molly couldn't help but focus on one word in particular. "Crosshairs?"

He pulled into the small parking lot of the bakery, slid his car into a spot, and turned to face her. "I'm sorry, baby. I didn't think they were still following me so closely. I hadn't heard from the government or gotten any threats from the mafia for more than a year. I'd thought they'd moved on from me or I would have never come to visit you."

Her hands were trembling, her heart pounding.

Crosshairs. Following. Government. Mafia. Threats.

It should have been the starting plot for a movie.

Instead, it had been Jackson's life for the last four years.

"Baby." He cupped her cheek. "Please know—"

She turned her head, met his chocolate eyes that looked so dark in the shadowed dimness of the early morning. "Why are you here?" she asked.

He frowned. "I—"

"No, I mean, today. *Now*. Why are you here this morning?"

"I need to be where you are."

Simple words she once would have given anything to hear. But now they seemed to have a different meaning.

"Because I'm in danger?"

He nodded.

Unbidden, her heart sank. "I see." She reached for her purse, slung it over one shoulder. "Let's go in. I can't get behind." She pushed out of the car, her travel carafe still in her hand, the contents untouched, but her brain all too awake.

More danger.

More martyring.

Only this time, instead of leaving, Jackson had forced himself to come back.

Being forced to spend time with a woman he'd left behind.

Every. Girl's. Dream.

She extracted her keys as she walked to the back door, slipping them into the lock, pulling open the heavy metal panel, pretending not to notice that Jackson was right behind her, his body inches from hers, the smell of cinnamon and mint tangling in her nose, her spine tingling with the urge to allow herself to melt back and lean against his hard chest.

Instead, she punched the code for the alarm, waited for him to trail her in, then hit the dead bolt she'd installed after he'd shown her the picture a month before.

Yes, *she'd* installed it. She'd gotten good with a drill over the years, and while she knew the lock wasn't foolproof, that it wasn't even the door through which the photograph was taken, it still gave her some peace of mind. No one was getting through the back door.

She stashed her purse in her office, grabbed an apron from the hook in the kitchen, then placed her phone in the cradle to start her morning playlist of whatever was upbeat and pop and could help her channel sweet and light vibes.

Because it reflected in sweet and light pastry dough.

Lie.

But also, she was the boss, her baked goods were the shit, and thus no one was going to argue with her. She got to listen to her saccharine music. She got to bake. And everyone else got to eat.

The fast beat blared to life through the wireless speakers as she washed her hands and started gathering ingredients.

Flour. Eggs. Yeast. Butter. Milk—

The music stopped.

She spun. Seriously? The man was invading her life. Not because he wanted her—not that *she* wanted *him* either, but still! He'd waylaid her outside her duplex, had bustled her to his car, and was only here because he felt guilty for bringing something down on her that he didn't have any control over.

"Why are you pissed?"

Molly froze. "Why am I pissed? *Why am I pissed?*" She threw her hands up, began weighing out flour into the giant stainless-steel bowl in front of her. "Oh, I don't know, maybe because my ex-fiancé has popped back into my life twice now in a month, after not seeing him for *years*. And only because he was pissed that I wanted him out of *my* life for good." She shook a little more flour out, checked the weight. "Or *maybe* that my ex just declared that he's staying around because he's got a misguided notion that he can protect me? Did you take a super-hero military man course in the time we've been apart and can now go Captain America on any bad guys who might bother me?"

She set the bag of flour to the side, moved on to the yeast and milk, warming the latter, allowing the former to soak in the warm liquid while continuing to measure the remainder of the ingredients.

"No."

"So, what makes you think that you can protect me better than I can protect myself?"

Silence.

"I'll hire some security," she snapped. "Up our actual system here, take stronger precautions, but I don't need you, Jackson."

And she most especially didn't need him just because he felt obligated to protect her.

Once everything was weighed out, she went over and started the music again then headed to the sink to wash her hands for a second time.

Good hygiene was important.

But just as she'd picked up a knife to start cutting butter, the music cut off again.

Was he fucking kidding?

She slammed the knife down, spun to face him.

He came very close. "Still not sure why you're pissed, sweetheart."

"You—"

He bent. "The agent said I needed to be here, and I'm going to be. End of story."

The *agent* said he needed to be there.

Her heart pulsed with pain, but fury quickly trailed that pain. Jackson shouldn't be able to have this power over her. She shouldn't feel so much longing toward this man who'd broken her. And yet, it was there. Because no matter how much she fought it, an invisible thread tied them together.

Or at least tied her to him.

Because apparently, Jackson was only here out of some misguided notion of duty and because some government agent told him he should be.

They were over. Done. Four years and gone. Finished. Out

of her business with a spectacular goodbye fuck included as a Happy Meal prize.

Now she just needed to take a hacksaw to that thread and get him to leave.

And *then* she needed to bake some fucking rolls.

Jackson dropped his hands to her waist, jostled her lightly. She glanced up, had to force herself to not get lost in the melted chocolate of his eyes. "You can be pissed all you want. You can argue and launch your cookie sheets—"

"Sheet pans," she snapped, smacking his hands away and stepping back. "Or baking sheets, not cookie—"

A flash of white teeth, but he didn't reach for her again, just crossed his arms and leaned against the counter, seeming so calm and composed when she felt like there was a tornado exploding to life within her. "You can launch your *sheet pans* at my head all you want, but I'm not leaving."

She was tempted to go find a sheet pan, just so she could take him up on the offer. "I've heard that before." A beat. "Or no, I guess I actually *haven't* heard it because we never got to the *till death do us part* portion of the festivities."

Chocolate eyes cooled. Hardened. "I didn't want that."

"I know!" She slammed her hands down on the table, nearly upsetting the bowl of flour and not caring in the least.

"I *don't* think you know," he murmured. "I don't think you believe me when I say that not showing up at that church was the hardest thing I've ever done in my life. That I wanted nothing more than you—"

"Except, you *didn't!*" she screamed. "Because if you'd really wanted me then you would have come, or you would have *talked* to me earlier. You could have explained. You c-could—" She stopped talking, dropped her gaze to the flour, and focused on breathing, on just . . . breathing.

No tears.

No more fucking tears.

"I should have talked to you."

Molly snorted then started dumping ingredients into the industrial mixer. Flour in, salt in one corner, eggs, the milk, and bloomed yeast. Each part coming together, each part doing its job, each—

"I—"

She flicked the knob, drowning out the rest of Jackson's sentence.

Which was just as well. Because that tornado was still spinning inside her, upsetting all the carefully built structures within her—the confidence she'd laid brick by brick, the insecurities she'd buried deep, the—

He turned off the mixer.

She saw red, fingers came up to grab the bowl, but instead of launching it at his head like she really wanted to, Molly walked a few feet and chucked it into the sink.

"You don't understand—"

And that was when she lost it.

"I have a fucking job to do!" she screamed. "Why can't you understand that? Maybe the job isn't something you think is valuable, but I do, and I'm going to do it without you interfering. Okay? *Okay?* Or is that too much for me to ask, you arrogant, egotistical, selfish bastard—"

"I'm not leaving," he said and crossed his arms, jaw tight, stubborn expression on his face.

"Fine." She tossed her hands up. "Fine! But I have shit I need to do. Things you're preventing me from finishing because you're in my face and turning off my music and mixer. If you want to park your ass at one of my tables, fine. Then *park* it." She forced herself to take a breath. "Just stop sabotaging my business, shut your fucking mouth, and let me do *my* fucking job."

His expression went unfathomable. "You've changed."

She rolled her eyes. "Real shocker there. People grow and change and—"

"No, you've changed because of me."

A sigh. "No, Jackson. I changed for *me*. I changed because I realized I wasn't fully formed, that I couldn't truly be a partner in anything—in business, in love, in friendship—unless I finally became my own person." She turned the mixer back on. "So, kudos to you for making that happen," she said over the noise.

"I'm sorry for my part in it. Sorry for all the mistakes I made." He moved toward her, but this time didn't touch the mixer. "I've changed, too. I wasn't fully formed, either. I was a taker and as much as I would have loved to make you my wife, I would have drained you dry."

Her breath caught.

His fingers brushed lightly over her cheek. "I didn't— I'm glad I didn't have the chance."

He stepped back. "I'll be here for as long as the threat is. And then I'll excise myself from your life as painlessly as possible."

That didn't sound painless.

It sounded horrible.

But by the time she realized that, he'd turned, flicked on the music, then picked up a messenger bag she hadn't seen him carry in and slipped out to the front of house.

The lights flicked on.

Her heart pulsed to the beat of the music.

But today, it didn't make her feel light and sweet.

And neither were her rolls.

In fact, she had to throw the whole batch out and start again.

TEN

Jackson

WELL, no one could say he hadn't deserved the verbal lashing that Molly had dished out.

He did and then some.

His only hope was that she'd gotten out the hurt, that she'd heard his apology, that they could navigate their way forward.

Because while he was impressed with the woman who'd built this place, who'd now opened two additional locations to much success, that angry female who'd unloaded on him in the kitchen wasn't anything like the Molly he'd fallen in love with.

She was more.

And yet, he knew that if she couldn't let go of what had happened between them, they had no hope of moving forward.

They couldn't keep rehashing and tearing each other apart.

They needed to navigate new terrain.

Which meant that *he* needed to help her see they could have something great between them again. That it might not be the same as what they'd had, but that it could be more and wonderful and—

His cell rang.

He glanced at the screen, saw that the number was Dan's, and picked up. "Yeah?"

A beat of hesitation, then, "You okay?"

Pinning his phone between his shoulder and ear, he began pulling out the things he'd need to work from Molly's shop—laptop, mobile hotspot (since he couldn't trust his business to an unsecured WIFI network), pad and paper (because sometimes his mind worked better via old school methods)—and replied, "Fine. What did you need?"

Another pause. This time longer.

"What, Plantain? I've got shit to do—"

"That was a pretty intense fight," he said. "I just wanted to make sure—"

Jackson almost dropped his phone. "You were inside?"

"No. I . . ." He sighed. "We have eyes and ears inside the bakery. Just to make sure—"

Dan kept talking, but Jackson stopped listening, or stopped *actively* listening, because he was replaying the fight with Molly, hearing the soundtrack of what she'd said, what *he'd* said, and wondering how many fucking people had just heard them airing their shit.

And fuck, did they have eyes and ears in Molly's office? Had they seen them?

"How long?" he asked, not giving a shit that he'd interrupted.

"What?"

"How long have you been surveilling her here?"

"Since last night. The team put them in while I came to your office," Dan said. "There was an active threat, and—"

Jackson stifled his sigh of relief.

They might have heard and seen him getting yelled at, but

at least they hadn't seen Molly when they'd been together in her office.

"I understand," he said. "It's smart, but I need to tell Molly. I promised her I wouldn't keep any secrets, and I'm going to keep my word."

"I was afraid you'd say that," Dan told him. "I get it, man, I really do. But know if she freaks out and has us take the audio and visual out then we won't be able to protect her properly, or *you* for that matter."

Jackson didn't have a death wish, but his well-being was much lower on his priority list than making sure whatever risk had bled over from his life into Molly's was taken care of.

He wanted her safe.

He wanted her happy.

He wanted to figure out a way to move forward.

"I'll do my best to help her understand that it's important for her safety," he said. "And temporary."

"Temporary is a good point to focus on," Dan said. "That and chocolate—" He broke off. "Okay, she probably has plenty of chocolate. How about alcohol? Or really expensive shoes?"

"Alcohol and kitchen accessories are my safest best, I think," he muttered, hitting the button to boot up his laptop. "The woman can never turn away from a new spoon."

A beat, then, "Kinky."

Jackson snorted. "So, were you just calling me for a heart-to-heart, or did you actually have something important to discuss?"

"Heart-to-heart."

He rolled his eyes. "Cool. Well, some of us have real work to do."

"I resent that comment," Dan said, then his voice went serious. "One of us will always be watching, and listening, and close. We'll send in the troops if something goes down."

Fuck, that didn't sound good.

"Do you think something is going to go down here?"

Because fuck what he'd said about not interfering with Molly's business. If she were at more risk here, if the bakery were targeted, then he was bundling her ass up and shipping her off to Alaska.

"No," Dan said. "They'd be stupid to risk something at the bakery. There are too many neighbors, too much cross-traffic. They'd be much more likely to make a grab at her duplex, since it's a corner unit and semi-isolated." He paused for a second. "Probably also something you should talk to her about. Think she would stay at your place? It's more secure."

No. She wouldn't like staying with him at all, but he didn't say that, just entered his password into the laptop's lock screen, and said, "I'll find a way to make it happen."

"Booze and kitchen accessories."

"Right," he muttered.

"This will all be over soon," Dan said. "Just remember that."

———

He'd placed his online order for the local kitchen store, along with one for the local wine shop, and he'd arranged for his assistant to pick both up and bring them to him by lunchtime.

He might have actually gotten off cheaper if he'd been looking to buy Molly expensive shoes or purses because, turned out, kitchen shit was expensive.

Or at least the brand he'd remembered her liking was.

Anyway, the collection of spoons and scrapers (not spatulas, because he'd at least learned *that* minimum piece of information from Molly during their time together), came bundled together like a bouquet of flowers. But apparently the wooden handles were *"to die for,"* according to the reviews, and he knew she'd appreciate the bright and cheerful display of llamas printed on the silicone head of the scraper.

The wine was just that. Something else she'd appreciate.

A medium-bodied Pinot Noir with fruity tones they'd discovered while wine tasting years before.

Once, it had been her favorite.

Today, he hoped she wouldn't launch it at his head.

A little after six, Molly came out of the kitchen with a tray in her arms and started filling the case.

Jackson hadn't consciously moved, but one second, he was in his seat, and the next he was at her side, lifting the tray—the *sheet pan*—from her arms and holding it so she could arrange the case. And when the sheet was empty, he pushed through into the kitchen, set it on the counter, and retrieved two more trays filled with muffins. Molly murmured "thanks" when he reappeared with them, but otherwise they didn't speak as she carefully filled the display case with the variety of treats she had managed to whip up in just under two hours.

When he carried the last of the empty pans into the kitchen, he came out to find she'd moved toward the front door, scooping up a newspaper that had been dropped through the slot, and was carefully folding it. With a look rife with different emotions —fear, tentativeness, frustration, hope—in his direction, she had set it on Ronnie's table.

"Coffee?" she asked.

He nodded.

"Have a seat," she said. "I'll bring it out."

And she had, along with a banana chocolate chip muffin that had him seeing stars it was so delicious. But then again, she'd probably known that, considering she'd remembered bananas and chocolate were his kryptonite. However, before he could thank her for the food and the coffee—also made exactly as he'd preferred—the morning rush began. Jackson had pretended to keep his eyes on his laptop, but in reality, he'd watched Molly as she worked.

In reality, he couldn't *stop* watching her.

Her personality filled the space with comfort, with caring. She had a bright smile and a kind word for everyone who walked through the door, and he knew it wasn't an act. He knew she *did* care.

She wanted her customers to have full bellies and satisfied taste buds.

She wanted them to feel comfortable enough to linger.

She was the lifeblood of the space. The reason it was so successful.

So, his eyes might have started on his laptop screen, but they'd drifted up to the counter more often than not.

Which meant his emails piled up.

It almost meant that he couldn't find the strength to care.

Ronnie, the older man he'd met last month, strode in, stopping at the counter to order, even though Molly clearly knew what he wanted. She'd had it over to him about ten seconds after Ronnie had sat down at the table with a placard of his name on it. The nameplate was new, apparently, and because it adorned the table next to the one Jackson had chosen, Ronnie told him all about how Miss Molly spoiled him and how she was so wonderful.

"There's a woman who shouldn't be single," Ronnie said.

"She's not," Jackson blurted.

Rather stupidly. Okay, *exceptionally* stupidly.

Ronnie's eyebrows lifted, but just as Jackson was about to blurt out something else, something along the lines of he'd fucked up and was trying to get Molly back, Ronnie nodded, picked up his paper, flicked it open, and said, "Good." Then he began reading.

Feeling like he should clarify, Jackson opened his mouth. "I—"

"No disrespect, son, but I don't come into this place to talk. I want to read my paper in peace."

Jackson's teeth clicked together.

Hadn't come in to talk?

This from the man who'd spent the last five minutes waxing poetic about Molly? Who'd talked his ear off during his last visit? Ronnie ignored him, eyes on the paper as he carefully turned the page. Okay, then. Jackson turned back to his computer, clicked to open a random email in his inbox, and started reading—

"My Molly deserv‍   "‍ ‍take care of her."

Jackson glanced ‍   re of herself."
Ronnie's brows drew togeth‍   e could reply,
Jackson said. "But that doesn't mean I'‍l.

The older man's face relaxed, and he nodded approvingly. "Good man."

Jackson's eyes flicked back to his laptop. "Not sure about that, but I'm trying."

"That's about the only thing you can do when you meet a woman like that," Ronnie said. "You keep trying. You keep giving. You keep caring . . ." He paused, waited for Jackson's gaze to come back to his. "You keep on caring until they believe they're worth it."

He folded the paper and pushed to his feet with a groan.

"Only then will you know that you've done your job right."

ELEVEN

Molly

SHE STRETCHED HER ACHING NECK, taking a short break from decorating the row of cakes she had spaced out on the tables in the kitchen.

Breakfast had come and gone, lunch was in full swing—the newest chef she'd hired doing a great job of putting together the hot and cold sandwiches and salads that dominated the lunch menu. The only major differences between lunch and dinner were the prices—lunch was cheaper—and the portion size— dinners were larger. Well, that and they'd thrown a seasonal pasta dish on there in the last few months, but that had been her marketing and accounting guru, Shannon's idea. She'd stumbled across a fresh pasta shop a few blocks over, and when Molly had tasted the offerings, she'd known they would need to feature their pasta.

So now there was fresh, bulk pasta for purchase in the case and a pasta dish on the dinner menu.

That was part of why she loved this city—the nooks and

crannies, the hole-in-the-wall restaurants, the food that never failed to make her moan in pleasure.

It fed her soul.

Just like this row of cakes was going to feed the bakery's bank account.

She stretched again, ignored the ache in her shoulders and neck, and picked up the edible flowers, choosing the prettiest ones and carefully arranging them on each of the white buttercream frosted round cakes.

That done, she gave everything a final inspection, boxed the cakes, and then carried them over to the walk-in. A few seconds to make sure everything was labeled correctly for the pickup that would happen after she left for the day, and she was done.

Well, with the cakes at any rate.

She had to start another batch of soup simmering, bake off the last of her roll dough, and check that her food order was ready to be sent off for delivery the next day.

Then she was done.

Sighing, she dropped her head forward, taking just one more moment to stretch the ache, enjoying the cool air of the walk-in, then straightened and reached for the soup ingredients.

Warm hands on her neck.

Jackson's warm hands on her.

"Sorry," he murmured, when she jumped and squawked. "I didn't mean to startle you."

"It's okay," she whispered, stilling as his fingers began massaging.

Frankly, *anything* was okay if he continued to rub the aching soreness out of her neck and shoulders. For the most part, she was used to bending over for hours, but that didn't mean she didn't still hurt when it came to the end of the day. Especially when she'd given up sitting on the stool because she couldn't reach properly. Frankly, her back needed a break.

"Those are beautiful," he said, voice still soft, warm breath hitting her nape.

"Mmm," was all she could muster.

The man knew her body, could hit every spot, soothe every ache, and while this massaging was what got her into trouble last time, she didn't pull away. Instead, she allowed herself just a few more seconds of the delicious contact.

Eventually, when the urge to spin in his arms and have him demonstrate the rest of his skills—only this time in a way that would definitely get her in trouble with the Board of Health—grew to almost a tipping point, she slipped free and grabbed the soup ingredients from the shelf.

She didn't protest when he immediately snagged them from her.

If he wanted to lug the heavy tub, fine.

Plus, if his hands were busy holding things, he was a lot less dangerous to her willpower.

"Where do you want it?" he asked.

Everywhere.

That was the problem.

"On the counter by the sink," she said, and if he caught the edge of need in her tone, Jackson didn't comment on it. Instead, he nodded and left the walk-in, and Molly would be lying if she said she didn't take an extra minute in the cool air of the refrigerator, trying to temper her desire.

Bad for her.

Jackson was very, very . . . good—

No. *Bad.* He was bad for her. He'd broken her heart. He constantly made her lose her temper. He'd said cruel things and shown up just because she wanted him out of the business.

But . . . he wanted to protect her, was here because—

"Because the federal agent told him to be," Molly muttered to herself.

The cold of the space finally penetrated her mind and body because . . . *that* was reality.

He wasn't here for her. He was in her bakery to assuage his conscience.

He didn't want her at risk.

But he also didn't want her—

Then why did he come back? her brain countered. *Why is he here rather than some burly bodyguard? Why is he lugging soup ingredients and massaging aching shoulders?*

Because they had chemistry. Because the sex was good, a bonus byproduct to doing the right thing.

Sigh.

Molly couldn't tell if that disappointed sigh came from her brain or her heart, but what she did know was that she had to grasp on tight to the reality that Jackson wasn't here for her, not really.

He was here for *him.*

Head on straight, keeping a firm hold to the truth of his presence, she left the walk-in. There was work to be done.

She'd best get to doing it.

"READY?" Jackson asked, just under two hours later.

She glanced up from the stack of order forms she'd been double-checking and saw he was leaning against her open office door. Since he'd clearly interrupted her while she was in the middle of noting something on the page, no, she wasn't ready to go. "Nope."

Her eyes dropped back down to the page, but her ears still worked.

Hence the reason she heard his sigh.

"What?" she snapped, eyes flashing up again.

"You're at twelve hours."

Her brows drew together. "What?"

"You've been working for twelve hours straight," he said, coming fully into her office and shutting the door behind him. "I haven't seen you so much as take a bathroom break, let alone stop for lunch or to rest for a few minutes."

"I seem to recall you rubbing my shoulders a couple of hours ago."

His lips pressed flat. "So, a sixty-second massage is a replacement for actual rest and nourishment?"

"I went to the bathroom," she pointed out. "Several times. And I ate."

"One croissant. Four cups of coffee," he said, crossing his arms. "Oh, and one half of an apple that was left over from the turnovers you made."

"I ate more than that . . ." She trailed off as she thought back. Hadn't she? She *had* started to pull together lunch.

"Your salad you made for yourself is in the trash."

Her jaw dropped open.

How did he know that?

"Because I just threw it away," he went on. "After seeing it sit untouched on the counter in the front of the bakery for three hours."

Damn. That salad was her favorite.

Kale and colored bell peppers, slivered onions, and a chipotle vinaigrette. And homemade—because, duh—parmesan crisps.

She'd been on track for a normal day, for a normal lunch, but then her employee, Todd, had been telling her about the new play he'd just landed, and telling her with a certain amount of flair. So much so, that he'd flung out an arm in dramatic fashion, and accidentally knocked over the gum paste flowers she'd crafted for the large cake order she'd finished earlier. They'd hit the floor, and what few hadn't shattered had needed to be tossed —because, well, they'd hit the floor.

Luckily, her client had been understanding, especially when she'd shown them a pic she'd snapped of one of the cakes with the edible flowers carefully arranged on them.

Vibrant. Elegant. Striking.

Something that was challenging to do with gum paste.

Something that nature made easy.

It wasn't the first time a kitchen disaster had struck, and it certainly wouldn't be the last time.

Nor was it the first time her lunch had ended up in the trash.

Stuff happened, she pivoted and coped, and made the best of it.

Then she got on with her day.

The final part of which was this order.

"Two things," she said, setting down the pencil she'd been holding. "Or three, rather. First, thanks for throwing that away." His face clouded, lips parting like he was going to interject, so she talked right over him. "Second, I know *you're* not talking to *me* about working long hours."

"I—"

"Third, I have to finish this order so that I can leave, and you once again interjecting yourself into my life is delaying me."

He crossed over to her, bypassing the extra chair as he rounded her desk, and leaned back against it, his thigh six inches from hers. Her stomach clenched, heat pooling between her legs . . . because this man breathed and she wanted him, especially when his eyes were hot and angry, his jaw tense. That intensity had always translated into pleasure for her.

And her body knew it.

God, she was so fucked up.

"Don't look at me like that," he growled.

She tore her gaze away from where it had been slowly drifting down, tracing the buttons of his shirt, sliding toward the brushed nickel of his belt.

But she didn't have to look lower to know he was hard.

Molly let her eyes clos⸺ ˙ˡy inhaling, and trying to reason with herself. A mon'   d thought to take control, to fuck him, to get her pl⸺   taste, and then they could be done.

They weren't done.

Not by a long shot.

Fingers brushing   cheek, drifting down her throat. Breath hitching, pul·   ing, lips parting.

"Are you going   ⸺ forever, honey?"

Her eyes flew op⸺   ⸺d Jackson was there. Right there. Kneeling next to her, his mouth so freaking close, his scent so overwhelming, the heat from his body so intense that she forgot about the order she was going over, forgot about her wounded heart, about the painful past.

She leaned forward and sealed their mouths together.

It was a spark in dry tinder.

Heat exploding into fire, into *need*.

His hands came to her face, angling her head, pulling her out of her chair and into his lap, her desk rattling with the force of him colliding back into it. But then his tongue was in her mouth, then he was kissing her like he wanted her as much as she wanted him, and . . . she forgot.

That she was in her office.

That this was four years after she'd been dumped.

That this wasn't her and Jackson and what they'd had before.

His tongue stroked hers, his lips alternated between firm and soft, coaxing and demanding, his fingers clenched on her hips. Molly moaned and reached for his chest, starting to tear at the buttons on his shirt, pelvis canting, wanting, *needing* to get closer.

Jackson caught her hands, tore his mouth away.

Unceremoniously stood then deposited her in her desk chair.

He stood, towering over her for several heartbeats, eyes blazing, chest rising and falling in rapid succession.

Then he dropped his chin to his chest.

Inhaled and exhaled one long, slow breath.

His head came up, face placid, though his eyes still burned. "Finish your work so I can drive you home." He strode for the door.

Anger flared through her, hot and furious and overwhelming. She wanted to snap at him for coming back into her life. To scream and yell and throw things because he'd shattered the perceptions she'd held on to as an excuse to keep the world away. His fault. It was all his fault.

Except . . . it wasn't.

She knew that. Logically.

It was just easier to continue being mad, rather than acknowledging that he might have had legitimate reasons for leaving.

Safer.

If she were locked down, then she couldn't get hurt.

But there. *That.* The slight dip in his shoulders as he walked, the way he was holding himself.

It was far too familiar.

Because he was hurting, just as she was.

And *finally,* she was able to look beyond the anger enough to realize that Jackson had been wounded, too.

Perhaps even more.

Because while she'd been able to burn him in proverbial effigy, he'd had to be the bad guy, the one who'd separated them, and not because he wanted to, because he'd been trying to keep her safe.

Should he have talked to her? Should he have looped her in and not just broken things off without thinking it through?

Yes.

But could she understand wanting to keep the Jackson she'd loved safe, being willir~   *nything* to protect him, even if that meant breaking his

Also, yes.

And was this anger t~   vas it eating her up inside so she felt like she was consta   'ge, always just a hair trigger away from exploding? Wa   \e with holding on to the fury?

Yes.

No, she couldn't just ˡ   all, pretend it hadn't happened.

But she *could* put it aside, help him figure out the situation that was putting them both at risk, and then move on from it.

Healthier. More whole.

"Jackson?" she called when he reached for the doorknob.

He spun. "Yeah?"

"I want to hate you," she told him. "I want to hate you so you can never hurt me again." Honest words, albeit harsh. Still, she knew that she owed it to both of them to also give him the truth.

"I know, Mol." He swallowed hard, eyes dropping to the floor.

"But—" His gaze flew back up. "I can't," she murmured. "I can't hate you, Jackson."

His chest expanded, hope exploding across his face. "Honey—"

Put it aside. Move on. Stop being angry.

Yes to all of those things.

But . . . saying yes to all of that didn't also mean saying yes to opening herself back up to the potential world of hurt that was Jackson Davis.

"I need to finish this," she interrupted. "Then you can drive me home."

His expression dimmed slightly, the hope disappearing, and she told herself that she would not feel guilt. She. Would. Not. Feel. Guilt.

She felt it anyway.

But she didn't stop him from reaching for the doorknob this time, nor from turning it and pulling the wooden panel open. Nor from disappearing back into the hall.

Enough anger.

But her walls were staying up.

TWELVE

Jackson

I CAN'T HATE YOU, Jackson.

I want to hate you.

Fuck.

His plan for winning Molly over wasn't exactly going smoothly.

But at least she didn't hate him, or *couldn't* hate him. That was something.

He was waiting in the hall outside her office, thankful that she'd introduced him to her staff after the morning rush as an old friend who'd be hanging at the bakery working for the present. Because of that, no one was questioning his presence in the staff-only spaces.

It had been twenty minutes since he'd retreated from Molly's office, only leaving to grab his messenger bag with his work materials that he'd stowed behind the counter, and then running out to his car before returning to lean against the wall while answering the slew of late afternoon emails that always seemed to appear when everyone was preparing to leave for the day.

The plus was he could do that from his cell.

The minus was that it was hard to type with one hand, because the other was holding the bouquet of kitchen accessories.

He'd met his assistant at lunchtime, stowed the case of wine in the trunk of his car, along with the "flowers" he'd just retrieved.

Paired with Molly's declaration of *I can't hate you,* he hoped that he might be able to make up some ground here. They had the chemistry, that was for damn sure, and he knew it would stay there even if her anger faded, because they'd always been good together. He was tempted to use that chemistry to his advantage. To keep pushing at her until she exploded again and he was able to get his hands on her, his cock inside her.

But that wouldn't solve the mess between them.

He needed her sweetness, the caring that filled the bakery. He needed her to trust him to not hurt her. He needed her to understand that he wasn't going to take.

He needed to prove that *he* could be the one to give.

So flowers, of the kitchen variety, anyway. Along with moving slowly and carefully, so that Molly would be able to trust him.

And make sure she was safe.

But Molly had been right about more than one thing as they'd gone toe-to-toe that day. He hadn't suddenly turned into a superhero. He didn't have the skills to keep her safe.

All he had was Dan and the security at the office.

He didn't have a bodyguard anymore, and he only knew that supposedly Dan's team had eyes on both him and Molly. Obviously, they would be easier to watch if they were together, and hopefully Dan was right about Jackson's presence being a deterrent since Molly was already on the mafia's radar. But he needed to figure out what else he could do, what other precautions he could take to ensure Molly was safe.

He'd been focused on the security of her heart, when he needed to be equally attentive to her physical well-being.

There was movement inside Molly's office, and Jackson quickly sent a text to Dan, asking him for some resources and recommendations he could use to protect her, money not being any object, then he pocketed his phone.

Molly tugged the door open, expression distracted, ponytail askew, eyes tired.

She stopped short when she saw him standing there.

"Oh," she said. "Um—"

He thrust the kitchen implements under her nose.

Not the smoothest transition in the least, but at least he didn't accidentally gouge her eye out with one of the wooden spoons.

"Oh," she said again.

"I figured you'd had enough with flowers today."

She glanced down at the cellophane-covered utensils, wrapped in a pink ribbon. Then her mouth twitched. "Llamas are a favorite I picked up only recently. How did you know I was into them?"

"I didn't." He shrugged when she looked up. "They just seemed bright and cheerful like you."

Her mouth fell open. "*You* think *I'm* bright and cheerful? I've yelled at you for a good portion of the two days I've seen you in the last four years." Her hand closed around the bouquet, one finger trailing over the pink patterned silicone.

He grinned. "Okay, maybe not around me," he agreed. "But you've created this incredible space, Mol. People love coming here because the food is good, but they hang around because you fill the space with warmth, because you give them a place they can gather and feel happy. I'm so proud of you."

Her eyes widened. "That's the second time you've said that."

"That's because it's true." He slid a finger under her chin, lifting gently when her eyes would have gone to the floor. "You're impressive, honey, and you've done a hell of a lot more than create a program that is equal parts useful and dangerous."

She canted her head to the side. "Last I heard, you'd gathered investments totaling over five hundred million dollars."

"Last *I* heard, the military threatened to pull out of our contract because I wouldn't give them a backdoor access into the program."

"What's backdoor access?" Her cheeks went a little pink. "I mean . . . in *this* sense. Not the"—she coughed—"why would they threaten to pull out—?" More pink.

Jackson's cock twitched, and he bit back a smile.

His Molly wasn't shy in bed. His Molly knew what she liked, and sometimes that did involve a bit of backdoor play. But *his* Molly outside of the bedroom blushed. God, he loved seeing that pink on her cheeks.

Especially when it reminded him of the pink spreading down her throat, across her breasts, over—

She smacked him lightly. "Stop looking at me like that," she said, echoing his words back to him.

He lost the battle with his grin. "Hard to ignore, isn't it?" He brushed a kiss across her forehead. "Backdoor access, in this sense, is a way into the program if they're locked out or someone has their security or privacy settings battened down. It would give them a key into anyone's data, at any time.

Molly frowned, opened her mouth, but at the same time, Jackson clued into the dark circles under her eyes, the fatigue dragging down the smooth planes of her shoulders, and knew she was so much more important than the latest crisis that had jammed his inbox full of emails and his calendar with conference calls.

"Let's get you home," he told her. "If you still want to know more about the program and can stay awake through the explanation, I'll tell you on the way."

"Let me just check in on the staff and we can go."

He wanted to argue, to batten her down and rush her home, to force her to rest until she didn't look tired.

But this was her business.

She'd worked incredibly hard for her success.

And so, he wouldn't piss her off by hefting her over his shoulder and carrying her out to his car. He wouldn't discount her hard work by presuming to tell her what to do.

No.

He'd   that for when he told her that she was coming back   artment, and that she was staying there until Dan told   as safe for her to leave.

A   en Jackson was going to tell her she *still* had to stay.

B   'd gone four years without Molly Miller.

H   oing without any longer.

* * *

PREDICTABLY, his telling Molly about her change in living situation didn't go well.

Thus, there wasn't any further talk of back doors.

However, there *was* plenty of talk of her threatening to disembowel him with the new spoons he'd bought her.

Thank God he'd stuck with blunt instruments.

They'd had a few minutes of peace, the time between him showing her the case of wine in the trunk and then until the point during the drive home that she realized he wasn't heading to her place—read: ten whole minutes.

Then she'd clued in. *Then* he'd told her she was staying with him and that was just the way things were going to be.

She'd responded to that appropriately: "Fuck off, Jackson!"

To which he'd replied, "I will, if it means you'll see some goddamned reason and stay in a place that's safe!"

Her lips had parted, eyes furious, and then she'd softened and shaken her head. "You're the most infuriating man I've ever met." Another shake. "You know that, right?"

He'd pulled to a stop at a signal, opened his mouth to say, who the hell knew what, but he didn't get a chance.

Molly leaned over the console and pressed her lips to his.

He was pissed and frustrated and worried . . . and hard as a fucking rock, b   ng to pass up a chance to kiss   ry one of the conflicted and   she made him feel at any given time.

Her tongue was fierce. Her mouth was hot. Her lips were demanding.

Her hands pressed to his chest, moved down—

A horn blared behind them.

They both jumped, and Jackson's eyes flew up just in time to see the light change from green to yellow. He hit the gas, slid through the intersection a heartbeat before the signal turned red.

Whoops.

Out of the corner of his eye, he saw Molly was grinning.

Well, hell. He didn't think he would ever understand this woman.

But if she kept grinning like that, then Jackson didn't think he cared.

THIRTEEN

Molly

OKAY, so she'd lost her head for a second.

Kissing Jackson wasn't exactly keeping her distance.

But also, kissing Jackson wasn't exactly *not* keeping her distance.

Which didn't even make sense.

Mentally shaking her head, she knew that a lot of the last day, the last month, the last year, didn't make sense. *She* didn't make sense when she was with Jackson.

Always a push-pull. Always trying to align her heart and body with her mind.

Yet, all she knew was that when he'd yelled at her, when he'd finally lost some of the cool veneer in telling her all of the reasonable, *logical* reasons to stay at his place—better security, easier for the federal agents to keep tabs on them, not surrounded by woods that she normally loved, but with the threat of the Russian mafia potentially coming down on her that could be dangerous (also something she was willing to go without for a bit in the name of her safety)—and yelled, she'd finally clued in.

This wasn't about *just* keeping her safe.

This was more.

And perhaps that shouldn't have made her heart leap with joy, shouldn't have made her frustration at the order fade.

But it had.

Paired with the wine and the cute llama spatulas, and her irritation had fled.

Perhaps, that said terrible things about her. That she could be bought, that a few nice words and kitchen utensils meant she would lose all the fight she'd gained over the years. Or perhaps . . . it meant that she could finally be a grown up instead of a spurned, heartsick ex-fiancé, and understand his concerns, know that they were valid.

And so, she'd kissed him.

It had seemed like the most expedient way to end the argument, especially since they'd slid to a stop at one of the city's interminable red lights. Though that had backfired as they'd kissed through the green signal and probably left a trail of furious drivers behind them.

Her bad.

Though, the kiss had been very, very good.

But back to more pressing matters. She turned to Jackson and said, "I want to meet this federal agent you're working with."

At the same time, he kept his eyes on the road and said, "If you're already pissed at me, you might as well know that the bakery had cameras and microphones installed."

She *hadn't* been pissed.

The news circled her back around.

"Um, *what?*" she exclaimed. "Cameras? Did they—? Oh my God, is there some video out there of us having sex?"

"What? No!"

"You said there are cameras and microphones. Oh, fuck, who's watching them? Did they hear—?"

One second Jackson was driving, the next he'd pulled the car into an impossibly small spot on the street, thrown the transmission into park, and then turned to her. "Mol. *Stop*. Everything was only installed last night. There isn't a tape or a recording of us."

Horror filled her as she remembered what she'd said, how she'd acted. *Fuck.* To think someone had watched her freak out, seen her rage at Jackson as she'd aired the dirty laundry of their relationship. "Where are the cameras? Are they in my office? Did they see—?" She saw his face change, knew someone had been on the other end of the feed, witnessing her throwing herself at him, casually viewing her losing her mind and all semblance control when he'd kissed her.

Embarrassment was a hot poker through her mind, and she covered her face with her hands. "Oh, God," she groaned.

"It's not a big deal," he said, carefully peeling her fingers back. "Nothing is saved. Everything is deleted after forty-eight hours. They just want to make sure they have eyes and ears on you, just in case something happens."

She glanced up into his chocolate eyes. "Do they really think something is going to happen?"

Because if federal agents thought she might be at risk . . .

Well, then this entire thing was much more serious than she'd been giving it credit for, and *shit*, now she wasn't just embarrassed, she was a little terrified.

It's the Russian mafia, idiot, her mind said snarkily. *You'd be a moron to not be scared.*

Well, moron or not, she hadn't exactly been firing on all cylinders since Jackson had reentered her life. Everything was mixed up—her emotions, her job, her memories, her future . . .

none of it was simple or made sense, and now her bakery was full of microphones and cameras.

"I need to talk to the agent," she said again.

Molly needed to understand everything.

She needed to stop freaking out about a broken heart and a canceled wedding and start worrying about the fact that the Russian mafia was interested in her enough that federal agents had put cameras in her bakery to keep an eye on her.

Now you're getting it.

Jackson nodded. "I'm sure I can arrange that." A beat. "Are you going to keep the cameras?"

"Or what?" she asked. "I mean, seriously," she added when his face clouded. "What's my alternative? I take them out and risk some scary mafia guy sneaking up on me? At least if the feds are watching and listening then I'll be safe."

She hoped.

Jackson's expression darkened. "I'm sorry I came back," he said. "If I'd just signed those papers. If I hadn't gone to the bakery—"

Molly squeezed his arm. "I'm guessing you didn't know it would bring me back into this."

He shook his head. "No, sweetheart. I thought they were done with me. They'd gone quiet for two years. Dan said it was all but done, and . . . it's stupid, but I just figured that with everything turned over to the feds, with my security team in place, that there wouldn't be any risk." A sigh. "But then Dan showed up at my office last night, and he doesn't show up anywhere unless shit is serious."

That sounded ominous, and she couldn't help wondering how many times Jackson had seen Dan, and thus, how many times shit had gotten serious over the last few years.

But she didn't get a chance to ask because Jackson kept talking. "If I— *Fuck.* I should have just—"

"Had the benefit of hindsight?" she interrupted.

"I *knew* better."

"The universal human condition."

His brows drew together.

"You're experiencing the universal human condition of wanting to change the past even while knowing that it's impossible. Reliving and analyzing and thinking back through every single thing we did, in order to try to make sense of how things turned out. I'm well-versed in that. I swear, I could have gotten my PhD in the process after you broke things off." His face clouded and she brushed her fingers across his jaw. "I'm not trying to make you feel guilty, especially not when you've perfected the process. What I *am* trying to tell you is that I'm not mad you came back."

He snorted.

"Okay, not *all* mad. I'm so incredibly furious that you didn't talk to me about this years ago. But I'm also . . . I don't know . . . understanding? Or, at least, I finally have some clarity as to why."

"Yeah," he muttered, turning his eyes back to the road.

"I'm also going to try to not hold it against you quite so much."

She saw the corner of his mouth closest to her turn up. "I think I've earned your anger."

"Well, *I* think you've played the martyr for long enough," she countered.

He'd just flicked on the signal, started to check for traffic, but at her words he turned back to face her, jaw dropping open. *"That's* what you think I've been doing? Getting some sick pleasure out of sacrificing myself for you?"

Molly shrugged. "I don't know what else to think, Jackson. Your reasons for breaking things off might have been noble in the past, same as your reasons for parking your butt in my shop now, for ordering me to stay at your apartment. An order I happen to agree with," she added when it seemed like he'd argue with her. "I don't want anything to happen to either of us, and if me staying with you for a little bit makes that more of a certainty then fine, I can stand sleeping on your couch for a while."

"You're not sleeping on the couch," he growled.

A roll of her eyes. "I'm not arguing with you about that. My point is, the reason you ended things wasn't because you were crazy in love with me and were desperate to protect me, it was because you felt like you needed to punish yourself."

"That's—"

"And you *continue* to want to punish yourself. I don't know why. I could never love you enough to convince you to let me in that deep." Her gaze flicked to her hands, to the faded burns, the scars, the callouses. She'd earned the hardened skin, had dealt with the stitches, pushed through the pain to keep growing. Her eyes lifted, found his. "I wasn't strong enough then to chisel my way through the barriers. I was dealing with my own insecurities, was too scared that if I did push then I might lose you."

She sucked in a breath, lifted her chin.

"The difference is that I *did* lose you, and I went through some really dark times—no matter that it was ultimately for my own good or to keep me safe . . . I get that. But, I'm also different now. And I don't want a man in my life who's only here because of a misguided duty." She took another breath. "I want a man who loves me as much as I love him."

"I—"

"Feel like you have a duty to protect me because you brought this down on my head."

"Yes, but—" He broke off, shook his head.

She waited for him to say something, part of her terrified that he might suddenly declare his love for her and that she might be weak enough to forget everything and jump right back into how she'd been in the past. The rest of her knew she was too strong to do that.

"I'm not here just because I feel obligated," he finally said. "I care for you."

I care for you.

Probably the only words she'd accept at face value in that moment.

But also, words tha

He cared. People   ere cared—a person cared for a puppy, or a stranger   in the street, or a woman who'd once held a piece of   , even as he'd kept the rest of the pieces safely locked

"I care for you   said and left it at that, not giving voice to the way th   sliced deep, so tired of being angry, of being hurt. "I v   you on our safety. Granted that you do arrange that i.   ith Dan," she added then paused as she considered her options. "I want to know everything that relates to me. I *deserve* to know that much."

"I'll make it happen."

Molly nodded. "Thank you."

Jackson's eyes moved forward again, his hand for the turn signal, but then he paused. "I broke something inside of you when I called things off," he murmured. "I didn't realize it before. I thought that I could just piece it back together and make everything all right again." A beat. "But that's not how this works, is it?"

She shook her head, another wave of sadness washing over her. "No, honey, it's not."

He swallowed. "And even if I manage to piece it back together, it'll never be the same."

Molly hesitated for a few moments before eventually saying, "Sometimes staying the same is overrated. Sometimes the pieces have to be broken in order to become something better."

"Fuck." A quiet curse, under his breath, almost not reaching her ears.

"I'm okay," she continued. "Everything worked out."

"Except, I broke something I should have known was precious," he muttered, "and you can't go back to what you were before."

"I don't *want* to go back."

His jaw clenched, the muscle twitching just in front of his ear the only sign of how agitated he was.

"Jackson?" she whispered.

His gaze flicked to hers, frustration in his eyes.

"I think we were both broken. Back then, I mean."

He stiffened, and she braced herself, instinctively knowing that she'd touched a nerve. But then he sighed, and the tension left him. "Yeah, I think we were, too." A nod, pain flashing across his face before he turned, started to check his mirrors.

"I guess what we need to ask ourselves is . . . if we're both still broken now?" She nibbled at the corner of her mouth. "And if we *are,* then can we find a way to be whole again? Or will that brokenness continue to chase us for the rest of our lives?"

His hands convulsed on the steering wheel, knuckles standing out in sharp relief against his skin. Then they relaxed, and he flicked on his turn signal, maneuvering out of the tiny spot and back into San Francisco traffic.

"There's one broken person in this car," he said, the words almost icy they were so devoid of emotion. "And I think we both know it's not you."

She inhaled sharply, opened her mouth to say . . . what?

But she never got the chance to find the words.

Because Jackson's cell rang.

"Answer it," she said when he glanced at her.

Relief and disappointment slid through her when he did as she said, when he answered the call over the Bluetooth in the car and began advising his assistant on rearranging his meetings for the following day.

Relieved because the conversation had been another heavy, exhausting, mind-melting one, and they'd had enough of those for one day.

Disappointed because she finally felt like they were getting somewhere . . . and because she might finally have the courage to *keep* pushing until she made it through his walls.

Until he told her the secrets he was holding on to so tightly.

The ones that made the shadows cross behind his sad chocolate eyes.

The ones she knew were the key to understanding both where they'd been and what they could be moving forward.

———

It took some effort, but Molly convinced Jackson to make a detour to her condo.

She needed to pack up her things, to get a change of clothes and her toiletries, and despite his promises that he'd have his assistant pick up what she needed, Molly liked the idea of a strange man going through her underwear drawer almost as much as she liked the fact that the mafia had somehow entered her life.

That was, not at all.

So, he'd made a quick call to the mysterious federal agent, Dan, letting him know what their plan was, gotten the okay, and they'd made the detour.

In. Out. Just the essentials.

It had all gone to plan without any hiccups until she'd asked Jackson to grab her Kindle from inside the bedside table.

She'd forgotten what was inside.

Something she'd gotten so used to that she barely saw it anymore.

But . . . there was a reason she'd never thrown it away. Because this was another photograph that had changed her life, albeit of one showing her and Jackson, him down on one knee, ring in one hand, love written over his face. Her expression had been shocked and partially obscured, her hands coming up to cover her face.

Jackson hadn't hired a photographer to take pictures.

Rather, a stranger had snapped it and then later had come up to congratulate and pass the photo along. A kindness for no other reason than to be kind. And Molly had cherished that picture for a long time, but then it had become a painful reminder, tucked into a drawer.

Eventually, though, it had become a distant memory.

A pang, and yet, not the agony it once was.

Although, it wasn't so distant with the man pictured, standing in front of her of her with a tortured expression on his face didn't slice across her heart.

Because she got it now.

"I remember being so fucking scared," he said, voice rasping as his eyes came up to meet hers, small smile on his lips. "That you would say no. I knew even then that I didn't deserve you . . . and yet, I couldn't let you go." His expression darkened.

"Jackson," she began, stepping toward him.

His eyes came to hers, freezing her in place. "Like now. I don't deserve you now."

"That's not—"

He dropped the picture back into the drawer, picked up her Kindle. "Anything else?"

She wanted to argue, to push, to demand her talk to her . . . but walls.

Hers, that was. The need to strengthen and keep them up.

But also, *his*. The impenetrable ones she'd never been able to find her way over or through or around. One look at his face told her all she needed to know on that front. His walls were still in place, and they were stronger than ever.

Maybe it was better this way.

No. It was most definitely better this way. Stay smart, keep her head down, continue moving forward. Right.

But maybe it wasn't better? Maybe they could—

A shake of her head, a stifled sigh, then Molly zipped up her bag, and said, "That's enough for now."

She meant the clothes.

But also maybe . . . she meant the two of them.

But also maybe . . . she didn't.

FOURTEEN

Jackson

HE GRABBED the case of wine from the trunk of his car, shouldered his bag and Molly's, despite her protests, then closed and locked everything up before leading the way over to the elevators.

She held the kitchen bouquet and trailed him silently.

Silence.

He'd thought he'd been used to it after the last few years spent working late in the office after everyone else had gone home then returning to a silent, empty apartment.

But he wasn't used to Molly being quiet.

Their relationship wasn't filled with long moments of comfortable silence, of two people sitting in quiet reflection or mutely observing the world around them. Molly was a chatterer —talking about her day, about her business, about a new recipe, about a news article she read, about a podcast he just *had* to listen to—and he'd loved it.

As an only child of two working parents, he'd had a lot of quiet.

His mother worked eighty-plus hours a week at the doctor's office she'd founded, and his father had traveled, so much so that he'd once received an award from his preferred airline for the most miles flown in a year.

Jackson had been used to doing things himself, had run feral and roamed his house and neighborhood, living off an obscene amount of peanut butter and jelly sandwiches while getting himself to school on time, making his own lunch, and oftentimes, his own dinner.

Oh, there'd always been food available, plenty of jars of peanut butter and strawberry jelly, multiple loaves of bread, apples, bananas, graham crackers. Plenty of snacks for a kid.

There just hadn't been dinner around a worn wooden table, discussing his homework over vegetables he'd been forced to choke down, someone to check that he'd brushed his teeth at night, or hell, even someone to make sure he went to bed at a reasonable hour.

He'd fended for himself.

Which was probably why he'd been so drawn to Molly in the first place.

She had been caring personified, thinking of him and his needs, filling the space around him with laughter and conversation, and meals were never in short supply. He'd fallen hard, latched on, and . . .

Sucked her dry.

The elevator opened with a *ding*, making him blink and blindly step forward, following Molly onto the car then pushing the button for the eighth floor. After a few seconds, the doors slid closed, and she sighed.

"What's wrong?"

Had she gone back to being mad about his high-handedness? Or was this something else?

"Nothing," she said. "Or nothing *new* anyway." The last was a quiet addendum, barely reaching his ears.

He turned, locked eyes with her, thought about pushing her for an explanation.

But fuck, hadn't he put her through enough? Hadn't this day been long enough for her? He didn't need to add his bullshit to her—

"It's that," she said.

His brows drew down. "What?"

"The wall." He didn't understand what she meant, and luckily, she seemed to read that loud and clear. "*Your* wall, Jackson. The one I could never get through when we were together, the one I told myself I would be able to eventually one day find my way around, or even if I didn't, then the one I was okay with being between us because I was too scared to push, if that meant I might lose you." She cleared her throat. "It's also . . . if I'm being truly honest with myself, even though I'm twisted into knots, even though I keep alternating between being terrified and wanting to push forward, it's also the wall I don't want between us now."

He clenched his hands into fists, considered what had been running through his brain, the promise he'd made to himself to tell her everything from this point forward. He'd already told her he was broken, so he might as well confess the rest. "I—"

The elevator doors opened, and, instinctively, he put his free hand out to prevent them from shutting, holding the metal panel so Molly could get off.

She took one step, stopped. "Um."

Jackson's eyes flew up from the box of wine he'd been concentrating on not dropping and he skidded to a stop, elevator doors closing behind him, his chest only millimeters from Molly's back.

Then he quickly moved in front of her.

The man who stood so casually, leaning back against the wall opposite, one ankle crossed over the other, smirk on his lips, outweighed him by at least fifty pounds, and while Jackson was on the tall side of average, this man had a good six inches on him. His black suit was expensive and tailored to his body like a second skin.

Which revealed a body well-honed and riddled with muscle.

Fuck.

Molly slipped her fingers into the waistband of his slacks, holding steady, even as her breath came in rapid exhalations he could feel on the back of his neck.

The man took a step toward them, and every nerve in Jackson's body went on red alert.

"Privyet," the man said, leaning toward them.

Russian for hello.

Fucking hell. Where was the security Dan had promised? Jackson shifted to the side, slowly backing away, nudging Molly away from the man, closer to his condo. If he could get her inside, she could be safe and call for help.

"Mr. Davis," the man went on, Russian accent heavy. He came close enough for him to smell the expensive cologne, see the fine stitching on his suit jacket. "My boss would like to—"

The elevator doors dinged open.

The man's head swiveled in that direction.

Jackson didn't look to see who was on the car, who'd inadvertently interrupted the man's sentence, and he didn't delay, just nudged Molly toward his door, shoved his key in the lock, and got her inside.

Wine box he somehow still held on the floor. The door shut. Locks engaged. Dead bolt thrown. Cell in hand to call Dan.

Knock-knock.

"Go into the bedroom," he ordered. "Lock the door and call—"

Before he could finish his sentence, a familiar voice penetrated the wood. "It's me."

Dan.

"It's okay," he told Molly, checking the peephole before opening the door enough to peek through the gap. When both showed no sign of the mafia member, he shut the panel, pulled off the dead bolt, and opened the door.

Dan slipped through, gun at his hand.

In another few seconds, the door was closed, the bolt back in place, and his gun was back in his holster.

He pulled out his phone, pressed a button, lifted it to his ear, and said, "Shit's getting spicy. Let's call in another team. Report back on their ETA." Then he hung up, glanced between Molly and Jackson. "Should we order a pizza?"

Fucking unbelievable.

Jackson shoved past him, going over to where Molly was standing, her face pale. He slipped an arm around her waist and gently pulled her trembling body against his.

"Who was that?" she whispered.

"That was Maksim Petrova," Dan said, "Underboss of the Mikhailova clan, and a guy you really don't want to meet in a dark alley."

"I don't give a fuck *who* that was," Jackson growled. "You told me it was safe to bring Molly here."

"It is."

Jackson snorted.

Dan pocketed his cell. "We have cameras along every stretch of the hall, in the elevators, the parking garage, the stairwells, and guards stationed in the condo next door, watching the feeds," he told them. "Plus, I was there the entire time, ready to step in if there was an issue and me bringing in another team at this point will mean double the manpower."

"I think a fucking mafia guy getting in the face of *my* woman is an *issue*," Jackson snapped and felt Molly stiffen. "He could have—"

"I'm okay," she said. "It's . . . I'm not going to say fine—"

"It's *not* fine," he snapped.

She squeezed the hand around his waist. "That's why I'm not going to say it's fine, but he"—she nodded at Dan—"said he was there, that we were safe the whole time."

Jackson forced his grip on Molly to stay light, when all he really wanted to do was yank her against him, hold her tight, and pretend the rest of the w ᵈ didn't exist. He glanced down at her instead, took a breat'   ᵗ his voice even. "That's what he said four year: fore I got that fucking photograph."

Her lips parted. A lon   ipping free. Clarity dawned on her face, and she lear   e more heavily against him, rested her head on his sh

And he . . . settled.

His terror at her b   e same space as that man, as *Maksim*, faded enough   ᵗ think clearly.

"If you want this over wiᵗⁿ then we need intel," Dan said. "We need to figure out where they're going next, how they managed to sidestep our net. If we can find out how high this goes, who's working with them in our government, then we can take them down." Dan came toward them.

"You've been trying to take them down for more than four years," Jackson said. "And it's not working. Give me one reason why I shouldn't just pack us up, fly us to some deserted island, and hunker down until the threat passes."

"What?" Molly exclaimed. "The bakery. I can't just—"

"Because they will find you, and they will do *anything* they have to in order to get you to give them what they want," Dan interrupted, blue eyes icing over. "And if you're in the middle of fucking nowhere instead of here then *I'm* not there, and your chances of getting you and Molly out of this situation alive are nil to fucking zero."

"He's scary," she whispered.

Dan's expression warmed, lips twitching. "I don't like the fucking Russian mafia. I don't like not getting the job done. I especially don't like not getting it done for four fucking years." He leaned back against the wall and crossed his arms. "And I *really* don't like people getting hurt or threatened when they're under my protection."

"I still stand by my statement of saying you're scary," Molly said, her voice wobbling just slightly, and Jackson knew she was forcing the lightness in her tone.

But he was still so impressed with her all the same.

He hadn't been nearly so composed the first time he'd come face-to-face with one of the Mikhailova, or the Vory as they were sometimes called. He'd been a wreck, and here she was cracking jokes with a federal agent, laughing when he stuck out his hand and said, "Oh, I'm Dan, by the way."

She smiled. "I figured." A beat. "So, *you're* the one who's been spying on me at the bakery and trying to steal my secret recipe for my rolls?"

Dan chuckled. "The mafia would be smarter to do that. One of my team bought a box of them yesterday. I'd be five hundred pounds if I had access to that recipe."

"If you can get Jackson and me out of this, you have a life-time of anything you want from the bakery on the house."

"Sweetheart—" Dan began, but cut off when Jackson narrowed his eyes at the other man. The idea of him posing a threat to the agent was probably right up there with him suddenly possessing some superhero skills, but the other man wasn't a dick. He'd cooled it on the endearment and said, "That's kind of you to offer, Molly, but I've always paid my own way."

"You just want to keep your six-pack," she teased. "Now"—she clapped her hands and pulled out of Jackson's hold —"Jackson is going to show me where the kitchen is. You boys are going to plunk your asses in chairs, and then we're going to figure out how to take down these mafia guys, once and for all."

Dan grinned then glanced from Molly to Jackson.

And Jackson didn't have to be a superhero to read what was in the other man's mind.

Molly was incredible.

Molly was special.

Molly was . . . *his.*

Something that Ja   ew he communicated to Dan, lack of superhero skills

Molly, not waiting   to point out the kitchen, started down the hall, and   did what he had to after his woman had worked h   for twelve hours then had faced off with a mafia man   by joking with a federal agent— he scooped her up, c   r against his chest, and told Dan, "Get on ordering tha

Then while the,   iiting for the delivery, the three of them hashed out a plan to keep Molly and Jackson safe while Dan's teams hopefully worked their magic.

Because they all wanted this thing done.

Jackson just hoped that during the process he could figure out a way to win Molly back.

Unfortunately, he didn't think he'd be able to do so without laying absolutely everything on the line.

The question was: could he man up enough to actually do it?

FIFTEEN

Molly

SHE WATCHED Jackson walk Dan to the door, the two of them continuing to talk about the additional security from the company that Dan recommended.

Apparently, they were a mix of former government agents and military personnel who specialized in tricky situations like this. Not at all like a celebrity seeking a bodyguard, which Molly would have probably ended up with if she'd done the hiring, but people who had serious experience in dealing with bad guys like the mafia.

The pizza had been delivered—well, picked up by one of Dan's team to make sure it was safe—and they'd eaten as they'd discussed the additional security measures.

Jackson was going to continue to stick close to her, working from the bakery so Dan's team only had to cover one place. They were going to hire some additional protection and keep the microphones and cameras in place. And she'd given over her keys so his team could install some devices there, just in case the mafia came looking and happened to reveal something useful.

She liked the idea of cameras and microphones in her business and home about as much as she liked burning a batch of rolls, but it was a necessary inconvenience and so she was going with it.

Some part of her kept expecting to break down, to freak out about the fact that, for all intents and purposes, she was being followed by the mob.

A scary, Russian branch of it.

And yet, she was somehow holding it together.

Probably because Dan and Jackson had looped her in. She knew as much about the ongoing investigation as Jackson—which was basically that they wanted his program so they could use it to support their illegal businesses by selling private information and blackmailing prominent users. But just as Jackson had refused to allow the government backdoor access to the data, he wasn't letting the mob have it.

He'd turned everything physically to do with that program —all the servers, the computers, the storage—over to Dan's group, and any work was conducted remotely, carefully shrouded behind some seriously intense firewalls.

She had to admit that she hadn't quite understood all of what Jackson's company did until that point.

She'd known it was technical, knew that four years ago while he and his team had begun garnering more attention in the tech world, that it was valuable. She just hadn't understood exactly how much so.

He'd basically figured out a way to glean tiny bits of data from users and to monetize that.

Most of the time it was fairly innocuous, like whether or not someone was thinking about purchasing a specific brand of shoes, or if they preferred a pug to a corgi when searching for puppy videos. But it could also be used to follow other user trends—was someone at risk of being radicalized or thinking about hurting themselves or someone else.

Information that was valuable and could save lives.

But also some intense big brother shit, especially if someone who didn't have their users' best interests in mind got involved and starting gleaning data that was a serious breach of privacy.

The program was a dangerous beast, but it was safe, and Jackson's company was focusing on other ventures—including several security products that consumers could use to protect themselves from just the type of data gleaning that everyone who was after the program wanted to exploit.

"Basically, the consumer product would have fail safes to capture and delete information that might put people in danger before it can be picked up and sold. Kind of like armor for your online habits," Jackson had told her when she'd asked him about the irony of designing programs that would counteract each other. "But I've learned that protecting a consumer's data is more important than me making a few bucks from selling it to companies or governments—"

"Or the mafia," Dan had chimed in.

Jackson nodded. "Definitely that. So yeah, similar programs are already out there. Maybe mine is more efficient at stock-piling data, but I also don't want to be the face of a company that wants to exploit people or their personal information. I want to be proud of my work." He shrugged. "So, it was a no brainer, we made the shift."

That had taken her breath away.

She didn't think she'd ever heard Jackson so passionate about something. Yes, he'd always been driven, wanting to make his place in the world, always seeming like he needed to prove himself worthy.

But this was different.

He'd changed, too.

And she began to wonder what it might be like to be with this Jackson, what it might be like to have this man want the woman she was now.

Because he ticked all the boxes—protective, honest, passionate, thoughtful.

If only he didn't have people willing to hurt him in order to get their hands on his program.

"I thought they were done with me," Jackson said. "It's been almost two years."

Dan nodded. "We thought they'd turned their attention to other things, too. But the Mikhailova clan was recently caught up in a big sweep in Spain, and several of the higher ups were arrested and jailed," he told them. "That's why we have the oh-so-pleasant Maksim on our hands now."

"He's expanding their investments," she guessed.

"Seems likely," Dan agreed. "Many of their assets are tied up in Spain. They need money."

"And data, especially blackmailable data, sells at a premium."

Dan tapped his nose in agreement then changed the subject back to their safety, and while she could appreciate that was probably the more appropriate topic at hand, it was also more worrisome.

It was much more fun to be contemplating the mafia's assets than considering how their expansion of them was going to impact her life.

Case in point, the conversation Jackson and Dan were wrapping up.

She should probably be over there, going over the final details, making sure she understood every single thing she could. But it was nearing nine at night. She'd been up since three-thirty that morning, and her eyelids felt like they had concrete blocks attached to them.

Relaxing back into the cushions, she let them slide closed for just a second.

Then felt like they'd barely closed when she felt Jackson scoop her up into his arms.

"Couch," she murmured, so tired but also knowing that she'd promised herself she wouldn't take his bed. "I'm sleeping on—"

"Shh," he said.

Maybe ⸺ weak, maybe she had just hit her limit on stressful sce⸺ the day, or perhaps the long, emotional hours had ju⸺ caught up with her. Regardless of the reason, Molly⸺ otest further. Rather, she relaxed against Jackson's chest⸺ er eyes close again, not protesting when he set her on t⸺ d tugged off her shoes then her jeans. She didn't even⸺ eep when he reached under her shirt and unhooked he⸺ ping its straps down one arm then the other before tuggi⸺

Her head hit⸺ pillow, blankets were tugged up to her chin, and she swam out of the fog of her sleepiness to summon a response to his hushed, "What time do you need to wake up, babe?"

"Three-thirty."

Then she let the darkness swarm back over her and sleep tug her under.

She woke up to her cell blaring too damned early.

But that was what happened when someone got up in the early hours of the morning . . . or really, the late hours of the night before.

It took her several long moments to remember she wasn't in her bed, her condo.

It only took one more beyond that to realize she wouldn't have her coffee.

God. No.

Coffee . . . she needed. She wanted.

Regardless, she slipped out from beneath the covers, flicking on the light that had her blinking against the brightness grumpily. The bedroom was larger than hers, nicer than her. Same went for the condo.

It might be nicer, but it didn't have her carafe of coffee.

Rolling her eyes at herself, she stumbled over to her bag, which was sitting on a bench at the foot of the bed then slipped into fresh clothes. A shower would have to wait, considering she'd seen what looked to be a dozen knobs inside the glass-enclosed space, and she wasn't fucking with all those knobs at three-thirty in the morning.

Knobs.

Heh.

Also, three-thirty brought out her inner innuendo.

Tugging on a sweatshirt, she slipped her feet into her sneakers, zipped to the bathroom to brush her teeth and wash her face then spent several minutes attempting to contain her hair in a ponytail.

By the time she came out, she was in desperate need of coffee.

But, it would have to wait until the bakery.

At least then she'd have a vat of the stuff.

Feeling marginally better at the thought of copious amounts of the glorious, steaming beverage, Molly quietly slipped from the bedroom. The plan was to text Dan, who would drive her over and stay until Jackson came over at a more reasonable hour.

Jackson hadn't been thrilled.

But he also wasn't used to the hours. He needed sleep to keep running his business.

So compromise.

Except, the second she strode out of the bedroom, she realized that his agreement had been a means to end the fight.

Because Jackson was awake and dressed . . . and he held out a cup of coffee in her direction.

She took it, sucked back a huge sip.

Then another.

By the time the caffeine hit her blood stream and she opened her mouth to tell him to get his butt back to sleep, Jackson had her carafe in hand, his jacket on, and he was striding to the door while texting someone—presumably, Dan, because a few seconds later there was a knock on the door.

Jackson checked the peephole then crossed back over to her, switching the mug for the carafe. "Time to go, sweetheart," he said and set the cup on the side table.

"You should—"

He cupped her cheek. "You're there. I'm there."

Her heart skipped a beat and she wanted to ask him if it was because he wanted to be, or because he felt he *had* to be.

However, instead of that question coming out from between her lips, "You know how I take my coffee?" emerged in its place.

Early.

It was early and she hadn't had enough caffeine.

That was the only explanation for the nonsensical question.

Jackson glanced down at her, eyes melted chocolate, and then he brushed his knuckles over her cheek. "Yeah, baby, I do."

Clink.

A chunk of her wall crumbled and hit the dirt.

Before she could focus—or in reality, *panic* on that realization, he grabbed her hand, tugged her to the door, and whispered, "Time to make some of your sweet treats, baby."

She was woman enough to admit the raspy words made her shiver.

Made her want.

SHE FELT him a second before he slipped the tray from her hands, holding for her as she filled the case with warm muffins—double chocolate chunk, raspberry with a cream cheese swirl, her ever-popular lemon poppy seed, and, though she wasn't admitting it to the universe (or herself) banana chocolate chip for Jackson.

It had been three d̲   she'd begun staying at his condo, and those three da̲   ᵓn filled with . . . right.

Jackson was there.

It was the same and y   ıt.

They'd always fit.   a few seconds of literally bumping into each othe   ̩T nearly seven years before, they'd fit. Numbers exch   ffee grabbed, movies seen and shared tub of popcorn   d. It was always easy, their bodies in tune in the bec̲   out of it.

And perhaps that eᵤₛᵧ, ...ᵉ way they'd slid into each other's lives seamlessly, how they'd liked the same TV shows and food, how they'd just plain gotten along from the beginning had hid the problems in their relationship. Because they got close and they did it fast and within a few short months, Molly hadn't been able to imagine a life without him.

She'd gotten attached.

She'd been afraid to lose that close if she pushed to delve deeper than he was willing to give.

So, they'd existed. They'd continued on that path and she'd been happy.

But after Jackson had broken up with her, once she'd lost that connection anyway, Molly had realized how unhealthy it was. She shouldn't be afraid to push the person who she was going to spend the rest of her life with.

She should be free to be her.

And maybe now she could be?

Before she could focus fully on that, he'd gone and returned with another tray. "Here you go, baby," he murmured, holding it up for her to load the next shelf. She glanced up, got lost in those chocolate eyes, warmed and shining down on her. There was something there, something different and open and deeper . . . and it gave her hope that—

The bell over the door tinkled, and Ronnie walked in.

"Go," Jackson told her. "I'll finish up."

Her favorite regular (shh, don't tell anyone) made his way to the counter, put down his traditional five, ordering his coffee and his lemon poppy seed muffin—there was a reason she made them every day, and it wasn't just because they were delicious and sold well.

They were Ronnie's favorite. His wife had made them for him and he'd had them for breakfast every day for the last fifty years of his marriage.

When his wife had gotten ill, he would come in and buy two of them every morning, packed up to-go, and take them home. But eventually . . . he'd come in and bought only one lemon muffin, then he had begun to stay and eat it while drinking a cup of coffee, his expression lost and closed down and . . . well, it had told her enough.

So she made them.

Every day.

She bantered with Ronnie, told him to grab his table, and poured his coffee, but then when she turned to grab the muffin, Jackson already had one readied on a plate.

He remembered the lemon poppy seed.

He remembered.

Clink.

Another piece of that wall chipped away, fell to the ground.

Although, this time it wasn't so scary.

"No!" She sat bolt upright in a cold sweat, heart pounding, head   and totally confused as to her whereabouts for severa   ·tbeats.

But   ·entle hand touched her cheek, a soft, raspy voice re   · ears, "It's okay, baby. I'm here," and she calmed e   be coaxed back down onto the mattress, to allow hers   ·cked into Jackson's arms.

Probab.   uld have moved, used her moment of alertness to go ot   · living room and sleep on the couch like she'd told hii   ; going to do, like she'd told him *every* night she was ţ   _g ţo do since she'd begun to stay here.

But it didn't matter if she got tired and drifted off on the couch or if she fought tooth and nail with him about not sleeping in his bed, she still ended up there.

Hell, just that evening she'd threatened to order a bed online to fill the empty second bedroom, but Jackson had argued he liked his empty room because it showed off the windows.

Showed off the windows.

What the hell did that even mean?

He'd just been trying to annoy her. And know what? It had worked. She'd flounced off into the bedroom, taken a long soak in his huge bathtub, and she'd crawled into his bed, eyes sliding shut almost before her head hit the pillow.

Tonight, however, she hadn't woken alone.

Tonight, she'd woken up with Jackson in bed with her.

And . . . his arms felt good.

Too good.

He was snuggly and warm, and she didn't want to move. She wanted to stay in his embrace forever, especially when he held her like she was precious and whispered soothing endearments in her ear. So words that made her forget all about the dream that had woken her, heart racing.

The fear disappeared because . . . God, she'd missed sleeping with this man.

"It's okay," he kept murmuring, one hand rubbing up and down her back. "It's okay, honey. Just sleep. I've got you."

"Do you want me?" she asked, and later she would blame the combination of his snuggly arms and the lingering drowsiness from her nightmare, but mostly it was just that she *needed* to know.

His hand froze. "What?"

"It's just . . . when you picked me up and brought me to the bakery last week, you said you were staying near me because Dan told you to, not necessarily because you wanted things to work out between us. Is that . . . is that still the case?"

Silence.

Arms slipping free.

Her gut sinking.

Then the light flicked on, blinding her for several seconds.

"What the hell did you just say?" he asked, gaze furious.

She sat up, tugging the blankets with her when she remembered she wasn't wearing a bra. "I . . . it's okay, Jackson. I mean, I get it if too much time has passed, and things have changed for you. I just thought . . ." She trailed off.

"Molly. What. The. Hell. Are. You. Saying?" Each word was clipped out, like raindrops plinking against metal.

"I just— I guess I was wondering if you thought that when this is all over . . ." Here she lost her steam, gaze flicking to his face and then away, but when he didn't say anything, she kept talking. "Um . . . I guess I thought we could see about maybe . . .

if you and I, these new, changed, *better* versions, might have something special . . . like we used to?"

She finally clamped her mouth closed, trying to not analyze the mess she'd just spewed.

Her cheeks felt hot, her skin too tight, her discomfort growing by the second.

Because Jackson didn't say anything.

Anything.

Know what? That couch sounded pretty good right about now.

She shoved herself off the mattress, took one step toward the bedroom door, and found ˡᶜ ᵗugged back against a hard chest. "What did you just   asked again, and Molly only shook her head in reply.   eady done the verbal vomit. There was no way she   ng back and repeating for a second round.

Thankfully, Jacksc   actually seem to need her to repeat it.

He spun her in hi   l said, "Are *you* seriously asking *me* if we can have ɛ   ɪot?" A hard shake of his head. "Honey, I'm the one   ld be begging you for that. I'm the one who'd planned on begging you *for that*." He cupped her cheek. "I just spent the last three hours ordering you llama-emblazoned towels and potholders, and more spatulas and a stand mixer with llama decals for my condo, because you've always liked it when your kitchen stuff matched, and that doesn't even touch on the llama pajamas and the grocery order for your favorite ice cream and chocolate-covered pretzels, or the bath stuff in your favorite scent—"

"You were able to find Bourbon and Strawberry?" she asked, which was totally not the important part of what he'd just said.

He nodded anyway.

"But it's discontinued."

The ghost of a smile. "I have my sources." A beat. "Honey, I spent the time looking for your favorite things because I spent this week hoping I just could get you to not hate me, forming a plan in my mind, a long, hard-fought quest to get you to just give me one more shot to make you happy, and then you just turn to me and casually ask if we could see where things go?" His eyes warmed. "*Fuck, baby*. Nothing like ruining my process."

She didn't take offense to the last because it was said lightly, his eyes teasing. Instead, Molly pressed for some clarification. "But in the bakery, you said that you were only staying because Dan told you to."

"He did advise that," Jackson said.

A sigh.

Because why the subterfuge?

He understood the meaning of her sigh without an explanation. "Because you were so angry, baby. I thought . . . well, I thought it would take ages to convince you to give me another chance."

Her gut tightened, and she let her eyes drift away.

She'd spent barely a week with this man in the last four years and had asked him to give them another shot.

Was she insane?

Or worse, had she gone back to the same pathetic weakling she'd been in the past?

But then she thought of the conversation with the first night in his condo, the way he helped out at the bakery, how he didn't minimize her work. Then she thought of Jackson staying up for hours, saw his laptop on the nightstand, the screen showing a page of models wearing bright, colorful pajamas, and she knew he'd spent time looking for things she liked, knew he was expending effort to show he cared.

And she knew this was different.

Being included, being treated as a partner, not something fragile to be taken care of.

She thought of why he'd done what he'd done.

How they'd both changed.

And she knew this wasn't old habits or the past repeating itself. This was a shot at something different.

Something more

Jackson d   :nd to not notice the internal war waging no doubt refle   :r expression. Instead, he said, "I know. I know I change   )etween us, that there is something irrevocably altered   l never get back, but also, Molly, please just know tha   has to be decided tonight," he added. "Let me take   hat quest to convince you to give me another shot. I   heart safe and secure until I've earned your trust back

He meant i

And that's .... finally believed everything.

"You know," she murmured. "I always had this complex when it came to how I compared myself to my family."

He frowned.

"I know you didn't know." She shook her head. "Sorry, I know that probably doesn't make sense. I just mean, I was so ashamed to feel inferior, knew logically it wasn't something I *should* be feeling, that I should be confident and comfortable in my own skin . . . but I wasn't." She sighed. "I knew it was bad to think that way, so I didn't tell anyone. Not even you."

"Mol—"

"Let me finish?"

He nodded.

"You know my family," she said, and he nodded again. "You know they're wonderful, that they never consciously made me feel inferior . . . but I still did. I mean, my siblings are so successful, and I didn't get into a great college. I wasn't athletic or popular like them. I loved to read and bake and stay home." She nibbled her lip. "And they didn't ever say that was a bad thing. My parents were supportive of going to culinary school instead college, bought me loads of books. I—I just never shook the feeling of being an ugly duckling."

"Your parents are proud of you, honey," he said. "They came to the opening and tried all the food, and they could hardly contain their pride. Anyone could see it."

"Except. Me."

He froze.

"I know we've both said that we've made changes over the last years, and I know we both meant it," she told him. "But my changes came from therapy. After . . . *us*, I went into this dark place, similar to this unhealthy place that I've spent the last week dipping my toes into, only it was much worse." She took a breath. "I thought you dumping me was the culmination of all of my unworthiness. I just *knew* that you were too good for me and that it was only a matter of time before you moved on—"

"That's bullshit."

She smiled. "I didn't say it was logical. It was fucked up thinking, something destructive I'd been holding on to and feeding for years, including the years we were together."

"Honey—"

"But therapy taught me that those feelings, as you so eloquently said, were bullshit," she said and touched his cheek. "It took me a long time to believe that, but I won't lie that seeing you after all of this time, confronting the feelings you brought forth within me, I backslid a bit." She thumped a fist on her chest. "I hoped. I *wanted*. But I wasn't free of those thoughts, of thinking that you weren't here for *me*. I went to the dark side again, even if it was just briefly."

Jackson gently placed his hand on her nape. "If I make you

feel that way, we shouldn't give this another chance. I don't want to be the one to destroy you."

The truth was there in her heart.

"Don't you see?" she asked, moving closer. "Don't you see that you don't have that power anymore? *I* took it back. Or . . . maybe you never had it in the first place, maybe it was always me, letting this self-destructive monster lose in my mind and heart."

"I don't know if I believe that, Mol." He shook his head. "I don't see how I can care about you as much as I do and let you risk yourself. I should back off, should—"

"And *there*," she said.

He frowned.

"There's *your* self-des   onster."

His eyes widened.

"Mine reduced me, s   of my wants and needs and accomplishments and pri   elf and my work into a tiny, damaged ball." She stepp   "Yours takes all of the good qualities you have—your l   r protectiveness, your ability to care and feel deeply   kes you fall on your own sword."

He inhaled sharply, and she wrapped her arms around him.

"I want to give us another chance. To see if we can slay these fucking monsters and move forward as something better," she said. "But, honey, you have to know your own mind." She hugged him tight. "I think you need to level with yourself about what you really *do* want, if the thing you truly desire is us in a real relationship. Or . . . if us being in a relationship again will just be another iteration of you sacrificing yourself for the good of others."

"That's not—"

Her cell blared, her very early alarm telling her it was time to head to the bakery.

She stepped out of his arms, reached for her phone, and silenced it.

"Don't tell me now," she murmured. "Think about it, and we'll talk later." His face darkened, and she hugged him again, tight and quick. "You owe yourself the time, honey. And you owe it to me, too."

His lips had parted, protest no doubt at the ready, but at her words, he stopped, eyes softening, and nodded.

Molly knew she was doing the right thing by giving them time.

What she *didn't* know in that moment was that later she would wish she'd heard him out . . . because *later* she didn't have the chance to hear anything from him at all.

SIXTEEN

Jackson

THAT DAY he was given a stool in the kitchen to park his ass, rather than his spot in the front of house, along with one half of a stainless-steel table he shared with extra takeaway boxes to park his laptop and cell phone. Molly kept the coffee flowing and the pop music blaring, but Jackson had learned his lesson.

Don't touch the volume.

Don't interrupt her when she was working her magic.

Surprisingly, being up at the ass crack of dawn wasn't terrible. He was definitely tired, especially after spending so much of the last week with minimal sleep and maximum worry, but being awake so early also meant he had a chance to actually reduce the number of emails in his inbox instead of just trying to tread water.

Being allowed back into the kitchen for more than a few minutes meant Jackson was able to step into Molly's office for a few minutes (and close the door to drown out the sound of Ariana Grande's latest), to take any necessary calls, as well as, to check in with the security company Dan had recommended.

The team he'd hired had joined forces with Dan's and was plugging any holes they could pinpoint.

They were safe.

As they could be.

The rest of the time—that being time not spent on the phone or managing his inbox, he did what Molly had asked of him that.

He thought.

It *should* be simple.

She knew how he'd grown up, that his parents had been uninvolved, but he could see how he minimized the impact of such a childhood. Any time he'd spoken of his past, he'd always framed it in the vein of independence was good for him—it had allowed him to think outside the box, to do things for himself instead of relying on his parents.

Now he wondered how much of a coping mechanism that was.

Instead of being pissed that his parents had considered their careers more important than him, he'd made the decision to think it was for his betterment.

Maybe that wasn't all bad.

He'd met plenty of people who'd blamed the world for all of their problems, and they weren't exactly pleasant to be around. So, he'd buckled down any leftover hurt, framed his vision for the positive, and moved forward.

That was a good thing.

Except . . .

How could it be a good thing when that buckling down meant that he'd hurt Molly?

That he'd craved the kind of love and care she'd given him to such a degree that he'd only been able to accept her affection, rather than reciprocate in any meaningful way? Hell, he hadn't been a total ass. He'd celebrated the holidays, her birthday, their anniversary, but last night had been the second time (sadly, both times having come in the last week) that he'd taken the time to shop for things that weren't necessarily expensive or showy, but rather, a few items he thought would bring a smile to her face.

Not buying something just because he thought it was the right thing to do, because it was what a man should give to a woman, but instead giving her something that showed he understood her, that he *knew* her. That he paid attention and cared.

And that it wasn't necessarily the right thing, but something that would make her happy.

She was right.

He hadn't been capable of giving her *that* before.

He hadn't been able to look past all the expectations for how things should be between a man and woman, between people who loved each other. He'd only been able to give what he thought was the right thing.

And the truth was that there was not *one* right thing.

Not a certain engagement ring or eating dinner together or having a career that provided for them. Not even her favorite ice cream or a llama-printed scraper.

Because nothing would be right so long as the wall remained.

If he held on to that solid barrier between him and the rest of the world . . . it would protect him, certainly, but it didn't discriminate. It separated him, just as effectively, from Molly.

So, yes, he'd hated breaking things off.

He'd hated not having her in his life.

But he'd also been broken.

Which meant he'd been able to keep a portion of his heart safely ensconced behind that wall.

So, he had to decide, did he take a sledgehammer to those bricks, did he punch a giant hole in the barrier, grab on to what he wanted, and let her in—*all the way* this time—past, present, and future?

Or . . . did he do what he did best?

Throw himself on his sword in the name of making her life better, while his remained empty and cold and devoid of anything except peanut butter and jelly sandwiches.

Fuck. That.

Jackson closed his laptop, rose to his feet, and turned to Molly, who was singing softly to the music as she measured out flour into a giant silver bowl.

He opened his mouth.

Then saw the red dot floating across her chest.

He didn't think, just moved.

The sound penetrated his senses when he was still too far away.

Pop.

"Mol—!"

A burning pain.

Darkness sweeping up.

Yanking him under.

The last thing he heard was Molly's ear-piercing scream.

SEVENTEEN

Molly

TURNED out that seeing (ɪncé getting shot was overwhelming.

Molly remembered sc. ᴄ nd dropping the bag of flour,
but she didn't remember the men flooding into the room, didn't
hear the yells and gunshots that left holes in the bakery walls,
had shattered glass and destroyed equipment.

All she knew was that she came back to herself when Dan
roughly yanked her off Jackson, shoved her to the side, and
began administering first aid.

She didn't even know how she'd ended up on top of Jackson,
covered in a pink paste-like substance . . .

Pink. Paste.

The flour. The *blood.*

She shuddered, tried to hold down the bile that rose
suddenly in the back of her throat.

Blood. So much blood.

On her hands. On her clothes. On her hair.

On the floor and the table and—

"Hey."

Molly blinked, glanced up at a tall blonde with startling blue eyes.

"Let me clean your hands."

She started to lift them, swallowing hard when she caught a glimpse of her palms stained with that mix of flour and blood, but then a pair of firefighters burst through the swinging door leading to the kitchen, and she was shifted to the side again.

Not delicately.

Not gently.

They needed her to move out of the way so they could help Jackson.

Which cleared her head enough for her to get to her feet, to make her way to the sink, and to wash her hands.

Soap and hot water, not looking at what was coming off her skin.

But then they were clean.

She grabbed a paper towel, dried them, then steadied herself and turned to see what was happening.

The firefighters, along with Dan and several men she didn't recognize, had surrounded Jackson's prone form as they worked on him. Stained gauze, opened packages, pieces of wrappers from the medicine they were using littered the space between them.

And all the while Jackson just lay there. Unconscious.

But still alive.

She *had* to believe he was still alive because they continued to work on him.

She had to—

As if Jackson knew she was on the verge of a mental breakdown, suddenly his head turned in her direction, eyes open and alert and riddled with pain.

Molly didn't stop to consider the ring of medical staff, the stained floors, or supplies. She just closed the distance between them and took up position by his head, bending and telling him, "You're okay. Everything will be okay."

His face evened out.

His expression softened.

But then his eyes rolled back, his chest arched off the floor, and she lost him.

Right there.

Someone coaxed her back as sharp questions and answers rang out, as more equipment was brought in, as gauze and IV fluids morphed into a defibril   CPR, a stretcher and then a rushed trip back out the   Jackson strapped to it.

Molly wanted blackness t   and claim her.

She wanted to go back a   t what he'd been about to tell her just a few hours befc

She wanted to demar   close the bakery and that Jackson haul himself off t   ored house where he would be completely out of reacl   afia.

She wanted . . .

Him to be okay.

"Mol," Dan said, coming over to sit next to her where she'd scuttled back out of the circle of healthcare workers, not needing to be moved brusquely this time, knowing they had needed the space to help Jackson, not her in the way impeding them.

But she also thought that perhaps she should have stayed.

Because Jackson had been so pale, so still . . . and she wasn't sure she would get a chance to touch him, his skin, his hair, smell the spice of his scent, see him smile, or watch those chocolate eyes melt.

"I should have closed the bakery," she said. "I should have locked him in his condo, not have allowed him out to put himself at risk, and—"

Dan set his hand on my shoulder.

"If we're taking blame, it falls on me," he said. "I'm the one who's supposed to be protecting you both, making sure you are safe. And I've done a shit job of that."

"Yes, you have!" she snapped, turning and glaring at him. "You *promised* it would be okay. You had all of these plans, and not a single one of them involved Jackson getting hurt or dying and—"

He tugged her against his chest.

Well, she didn't want to be comforted, didn't want to be coddled or held. She was scared and angry and . . . just wanted Jackson to be okay.

"Let go of me," she snapped, beating on his chest. "Let. *Go.*"

Dan didn't, just held her as she continued to struggle and said, "I could tell you all of the reasons why what the Mikhailova are doing doesn't make sense, that I've never seen them be so fucking careless or stupid before, that this doesn't fit their M.O.—"

"I don't care," she growled.

He slid his hand to her nape, tilted her head so her eyes met his. "I could also tell you that our intel is so fucked right now when it comes to them and how they're acting because the pieces we have are somehow fitting together and yet the puzzle they've formed is all kinds of fucked up." He shook her lightly. "I could tell you that we've taken down bigger and worse groups of bad guys and come out with everyone who we've protected along the way alive. I could tell you that I would have never knowingly put either of you at risk if I seriously thought they come in here again with loaded guns." Her gut sank, eyes sliding closed. "But—" He waited for her to open them again. "All I can honestly say is that I'm going to do everything to keep you safe, not just because I promised Jackson that, but because I'm promising *you* that."

"And Jackson?" she asked coldly. "What kind of promise can you give *him?*"

His expression clouded, and his eyes turned scary. "That we're going to take these motherfuckers down, once and for all."

———

THERE WAS a box of with a dozen lemon poppy seed muffins, Ronnie's newspaper, and a note for her favorite patron taped to its top sitting outside the bakery's front door. This was paired with a sign in the window saying that Molly's was closed for unexpected repairs

Lies.

But she figured it was better for her patrons to think a pipe burst or some ovens went down rather than knowing that there were bullet holes in her kitchen. Thankfully, Dan's team was handling the investigation quietly.

Not that there was much to investigate.

They had tape of the man entering the bakery, of Jackson getting up from his stool in the kitchen, glancing from her to the door, then sprinting toward her, and . . . going down.

It hadn't been him they were after.

It was *her*.

She'd demanded to see the tape, much against the advice of pretty much everyone, but eventually Dan had relented and shown her, and it had taken everything in her to not throw up.

He'd fallen to the ground like a sack of bricks.

Like a dummy.

Like a dead body.

Shuddering, she kept her eyes on the road, focusing on the traffic rather than those slightly pixelated images on the screen of Dan's cellphone.

She hadn't gotten in the ambulance with Jackson, hadn't

ridden to the emergency department. She hadn't been thinking straight enough for that. And by the time Dan had felt things were secure enough to drive her over, he'd gotten a call from one of his team that Jackson had already been taken in to surgery.

She'd still wanted to go to the hospital and wait.

They hadn't let her.

She got it, or at least, part of her did. Jackson had taken that bullet for *her* and putting herself at risk, acting like a sitting duck in the waiting room and making it easy for someone to come in and finish the job was not part of the plan.

Jackson was alive.

That was most important.

But it was absolutely killing her to not be there.

So, she'd spent the time cleaning up and shutting down the bakery then diverting the impending food delivery and outstanding cake orders to her other locations. Once the hour had reached a reasonable one, Molly had called her staff and informed them of the sewer line break—Dan's idea—telling them they'd work as much as possible at the other locations, but even if they didn't get the hours, they'd still have two full weeks of pay. While she was thankful she had enough in her reserves to actually be able to afford that without the business going under, she still couldn't believe she'd been focused on her business when Jackson was unconscious in the hospital.

Still, none of it had been distraction enough to completely erase the images of what had happened from her mind, what was happening with Jackson.

Then she'd gotten word he was out of surgery.

That he was alive.

That he was awake.

And she was thankful Dan had pushed her to get her affairs in order. Because her mind had needed the distraction while things were uncertain and because after the news had come in she wasn't in any way capable of doing it.

The adrenaline had faded.

Molly felt shaky and frightened and one push away from losing it completely.

Part of that was because she still had crusted, sticky flour in her hair. Her clothes were . . . ruined was probably the simplest description because even if she *did* manage to get them clean, she didn't think she'd ever be able to put them on without thinking of what happened.

Destined for the trash.

Just like all of her dough.

The rest of her just needed to see with her own eyes that Jackson really was awake and okay and—

Her phone rang and she glanced to Laila, the driver of the vehicle she was riding in, the blonde who'd kindly wanted to clean her stained hands that morning, and who was currently escorting Molly to the private hospital where Jackson had been transferred after he'd gotten out of surgery.

"Who is it?" Laila asked.

"My friend, Shannon," Molly told her. "She works for me, does marketing and accounting, and—" She stopped her explanation there, seeing Laila's eyes start to glaze.

"Go ahead and answer it," Laila said, flicking a switch on a box positioned on the dashboard. "No details of where you are or are going."

"Okay."

She swiped a finger across the screen, and Shannon's cheerful voice filled the airwaves. "I saw a missed call from you. Did you burn an oven full of goodies and need me to ride in on my white stallion and save the day?"

"There's been a sewer leak."

"What?"

"A main burst and flooded back into the kitchen. The whole bakery is shut down," Molly said, repeating the lie she'd perfected over the morning. "It sucks, but I'm going to take advantage of the time to tackle those outstanding repairs we budgeted for."

"*What?*" Shannon said again.

"Consider yourself to have the next two weeks off," Molly told her. "Let's touch base about details in the next couple of days. I'm too tired to break everything down again today."

"Okay, hun." Shannon's voice was concerned. "Are you sure you're okay?"

"Yeah. It'll all be fine."

She hoped.

"Well, I'm around if you want to come over later and share a pizza."

"I'll let you know, but I think I'll be at the bakery until late."

"I can bring—"

"What? Hold on a sec." She covered the receiver, made some muffled noises then got back on with Shannon. "Sorry, Shan. They need me to go look at something. I'll call you tomorrow, okay?"

"I—"

She hung up before her friend could get out the rest of her sentence, which was just as well. Molly had been lying all day and, sadly, they were starting to come easily, almost without having to really think about it.

That wasn't the kind of person she wanted to be.

She didn't want to be able to lie as easily as breathing, or to have to keep track of some complex web of half-truths.

And yet, here she was.

"You're doing really well," Laila said. "Most civilians would have fallen to pieces if they'd been through what you had today."

"No offense," Molly muttered. "But I'm not sure I want that particular compliment."

Laila grinned. "Noted."

She changed the subject. "How long have you worked for Dan?"

Brilliant blue eyes flashed over then back to the road, the grin widening. "Dan works for *me* actually."

"*Now* we're talking."

Laila snorted. "I'm just kidding. Kind of, anyway. We're more like equals. He and I both head teams. Mine is the one that was called in for extra support." She glanced into the rearview. "Though I am sorry to say that we didn't make it in earlier. Otherwise, the response time this morning would have been much quicker."

Molly frowned, not sure what she meant.

"Our plane was delayed because of fog, and we were just arriving at the command post when the cameras picked up on the intruder. If we'd been there, we'd have had more bodies on the ground, and he would have never got that far."

Molly's frown deepened, for two reasons.

One, it hadn't occurred to her to even think about the man who'd shot Jackson or where he'd ended up. Two, she wondered if the reason that they'd come into the bakery that morning was less about the Mikhailova breaking protocol and more about the fact that they'd somehow known reinforcements were coming.

Had they taken a chance to act before Dan's team had gotten back-up?

"What happened to the man from this morning?"

Laila scowled. "He must have clocked our guy on the corner because he slipped out the back door and got away"

"There wasn't anyone there?"

A shake of the other woman's head. "There was supposed to be, but he'd been knocked unconscious. Serious laceration that took sixty stitches and a handful of staples to close up." Laila scowled. "He's lucky he's not beside Jackson, recouping in a bed for the foreseeable future."

"I see." But what Laila told her made the hairs on the back of her neck prickle.

"What's put that expression on your face?" Laila asked as she steered the car off the freeway, coasting along an exit ramp that wrapped through a large grove of Redwoods.

Molly shook her head. "It's probably nothing."

"I've been in this career for too long to think that *nothing* is really nothing." She turned the car to the right. "Tell me."

Knowing it was unlikely she'd thought of something the agent hadn't already analyzed six ways to Sunday, Molly told her what she'd been thinking. "I just . . . none of this really adds up. First, why take a shot at me if they want Jackson to cooperate? I'm not trying to be an egotistical asshole, but Jackson doesn't have a lot of people in his life that he cares about, and if they killed me, I can't imagine he'd be motivated to help them."

"Go on," Laila said when she paused.

"So, I guess, I'm just thinking that piece doesn't fit. The killing me piece. Dan thought it more likely that they'd try to kidnap me and force Jackson to hand over the program. Killing me gets them nowhere."

Laila nodded, navigating the car up a twisting road. "Okay, I'd agree with all that."

"The other piece that doesn't add up for me is that maybe the Mikhailova's behavior this morning wasn't them being careless. Maybe they were told the team was coming in by someone on the inside and decided to act before that back-up came . . ." She trailed off, realizing that she was basically telling this woman she hardly knew that one of her co-workers might be a mole or, worse, a member of the Russian mafia.

Laila was quiet for a long time.

For a long, *long* time.

For long enough that Molly started to get nervous, to begin considering options for tucking and rolling and getting the fuck out of this car if Laila turned out to be the one who'd betrayed everyone.

"And now I'm wondering how all of us, how the people who do this for a living, could have possibly missed that." Laila gripped the steering wheel tightly as they approached a huge metal gate. "We've been chasing shadows, dodging and trying to capture an enemy that always seemed one step ahead. And not once did I consider that one of us might be helping them."

"It might not be that at all," Molly said. "I just bake for a living. It's not like what I'm saying is anything other than a guess."

Laila rolled her window down, punched a code into the keypad, and the gate began sliding open. "It's intuition. It's *logic*. And it bears chasing down." She hit the button to close her window, let the car move forward. "Because if what you said pans out, Molly Miller, then you may have just cracked a federal investigation."

"I—"

"Do me a favor?" Laila glanced over.

Molly nodded.

"Don't mention this to anyone but Dan or myself until we know for sure, okay?"

EIGHTEEN

Jackson

HE WOKE SLOWLY, eyes heavy, every part of his body feeling like he'd been run over by a train.

But then his thoughts sharpened, focused into one thing:

"Molly!" he said, voice hoarse, bolting upright in bed and then nearly collapsing right back down to the mattress when the bolt of red-hot pain shot through him.

Soft hands on his face, a beautiful face he knew better than his own. "Shh. Jackson, I'm here," Molly said, and helped him lie back down on the mattress. "Easy, baby. You're hurt."

He didn't give a shit about being hurt.

He wanted to make sure she was okay.

And that didn't have anything to do with the fact that he was being a martyr or sacrificing the things he wanted because he thought they were the right thing to do, that if he could be good or kind or brave enough then someone would love him.

This wasn't about the monster inside him—or in his case, the little kid who needed approval and understanding from his parents and then the world.

This was about a man and his woman.

A woman who'd had a red laser beam pointed at her chest.

So no, it wasn't martyrdom or approval-seeking. This was making certain that the woman he loved was unscathed.

"Were you hurt?"

"No," she said, hands running carefully over his face, down his arms. "I'm fine. But, Jackson, you're *not*. You need to calm down before you pull out your IV or something."

Frowning, he glanced down, saw that he was indeed hooked up to an IV, to several monitors.

"Where am I?" It didn't look like a hospital, not with the heavy drapes, the plush carpet he could see peeking out from beneath the bed, which definitely didn't look like something he'd expect to see in an institutional setting.

"Dan pulled some strings and had you moved to a private hospital."

His brows shot up.

"Yeah," she murmured. "Pretty plush for a hospital."

"Somehow, I didn't expect this of the federal government," he said.

"I know," she agreed. "When Dan said private hospital, I was thinking something more along the lines of beige walls and peeling paint."

"Exactly."

Jackson wanted to sit up again, to tug Molly down onto the bed next to him and hold her close, to physically feel her in his arms, to touch every inch, and reassure himself that she really was okay. But the burst of adrenaline he'd had upon waking was rapidly fading, and the pain was creeping back in.

"What happened after . . .?"

"What do you remember?"

He shuddered, remembering the red dot of light, how it had danced across the embroidered chest of her apron, but the shuddering had him wincing, and then Molly said, "Never mind. Just rest, baby. We can talk more later."

No. They needed to talk more *now*.

She needed to understand the shift that had happened in his mind. Who knew how much time they had, or if the mafia would come, guns blazing, into this hospital?

"I love you, Molly," he said, making sure it was the first thing he told her, in case the world imploded. "I loved you four years ago, but I *love* you now." He sighed. "I know that probably doesn't make sense, but I wasn't capable of loving you then like I do now." He took her hand. "You were right. I had something inside of me that kept me carefully separate from the rest of the world. It's just not a monster . . . it was a little kid, wanting to be loved first, by his parents, then by you. But at the same time, I was too scared to accept that you *could* truly love me, not when the people in my life who were supposed to do that from day one, couldn't."

She tilted her head to the side. "But you told me that you and your parents had a great relationship, that they had to work a lot, but—"

"I lied." He let his head fall to the pillows, exhausted, but knowing he had to make her understand. "I . . . they were neglectful. There's no other way to frame it. I wanted to call it independence or building character, and I pretended it was for my betterment." He laced their fingers together. "But it wasn't. It was for *their* betterment. Their lives, their careers, even their friends came before me." He squeezed lightly. "And I did that to you, when we were together. Partly because it was all I knew, a pattern to be repeated, but also because if *I* controlled our inter- actions, if I only let you into the carefully crafted pieces of me, then you'd love me and wouldn't leave."

Her face was soft. "Jackson, hon. We don't have to do this now. You should rest and—"

"No," he interrupted. "We need to do this now, because this morning I was getting up out of a stool, coming over to tell the woman I want to spend the rest of my life with, the woman I love more now than I ever could before . . . that she was right. That I'd been hiding." He lifted his free arm to cup her cheek, and it took way more effort than it should have. "And then I saw that dot on your chest, and I knew ⸱⸱ing knew that I'd missed my chance to tell you."

Yes, he was choked up.

Yes, maybe it was from the ⸱⸱⸱ ⸱ the injury.

But also, yes, it was beca⸱⸱⸱ ⸱lmost lost this woman again, and that was unbearab⸱

"You done?"

He chuckled in disbel⸱ ⸱arp edge of Molly's tone.

But that chuckle wa⸱ ⸱d because it was immediately punctuated by a groan. "Don't ⸱⸱ ⸱ke me laugh."

Her eyes flashed. "I wasn't trying to," she snapped. "What I was *trying* to do was to get the dumb ass man that I love to rest after he took a bullet for me, after he almost lost his spleen and then spent several hours in surgery to control internal bleeding." She pulled her hand free, paced away. "Internal bleeding!" she exclaimed. "Do you know how serious that was? How *scared* I was that I might lose you when we were finally finding our ways back to each other, and it was so *much* better than before?"

Hands on her hips, she spun back to face him and glared.

"Mol—"

Her jaw ticked.

"You love me?"

She softened, eyes gentling, fury disappearing from her expression. "Yeah."

"But Mol . . . you actually really do love *me?*" he asked. "The man who's kind of a wreck, who's only just figuring out that the way he's lived his life for the last thirty years was shit?

The same one who's going to have to figure out how to move forward without repeating the same horrible pattern?"

Her feet were silent as they trailed across the carpet, bringing her back to his bedside. "I love the man who ordered me llama-printed scrapers because he thought they would make me smile, the same one who remembered my favorite wine, who knows my preferred brand of ice cream."

She sank into the chair next to the bed, bringing their gazes more level.

"I loved the man from four years ago, deeply, irrevocably, but *this* man, the who cares about my likes and dislikes, who gives freely, who tells me the truth even when it's scary, and says he's proud of me, *this* man has the potential to be loved so much more deeply." She trailed her fingers over his jaw. "Because you're not doing it to punish yourself or alternately, dolling bits of your heart out bit by careful bit. You've given me *you*. And Jackson, I know exactly how precious of a gift that is."

He was frozen. Her words washing over him, filling him to bursting.

He was terrified and relieved, both in equal measures.

Because they had a fresh start.

Because he might screw up again.

He lifted his hand, cupped it over hers on his jaw. "I'll do my best to not fuck it up."

"Don't you see?" Molly leaned down and brushed her lips across his. "Don't you understand by now that neither of us is perfect? That we'll both definitely fuck up." Another brush of her mouth. "Plus, it's the making up that will be the most fun anyway." She straightened, smile escaping. "Only this time, I won't have to throw sheet pans at your head to test your reflexes."

Jackson chuckled then groaned. "No more making me laugh, remember?"

"I remember." A beat. "Only, I'm so funny, I think that's impossible."

He snorted but held back the laughter. "So, it's this easy? We just declare ourselves and move forward?"

"What do you mean?" Her head was tilted to the side in question and ridiculously cute. But then again, he found everything about this woman adorable, including her uncanny ability to throw large metal objects.

"We had all this hurt and history and bad memories." Jackson started to shrug but caught himself. "So, we just pretend it didn't happen and move on?"

"No."

He frowned.

"We remember it. We   back. We move forward and build something better."

"I can do that," he no

She propped her hea   and, resting her elbow on the bedrail. "I know you can.

"And you'll be abl   ?" he asked. "You're able to believe I've fallen back i   h you?"

"You took a bullet f   ie said matter-of-factly, though her eyes were warm. '   nink there's much clearer of a gesture of true love."

His mouth tipped up. "So, I could have just done that in the first place? Get shot?"

Molly sighed, shook her head. "You're an idiot."

"I'm *your* idiot."

Another sigh, though this one was trailed by a smile. "I'd take your brand of idiot any day of the week, Jackson Davis."

"Good," he murmured, lids heavy. "Because I'm not letting your brand of special go." He let his eyes slide closed, sleep beginning to close over him.

"Plus, baby," she said, sounding just as tired. "I think the truth that neither of us were willing to admit a month ago was that years might have passed, but we both never stopped being in love with each other."

She was right.

Though, that shouldn't be surprising with his Molly.

She had a knack for being right.

But then there was no more thinking.

Sleep tugged him under.

And the events that were about to crash into them would prove that Molly's knack for being right was even more honed than Jackson had given her credit for in that hospital room.

NINETEEN

Molly

FUNNY STORY.

There were contractors that specialized in bullet holes and blood stains.

Okay, so maybe that wasn't funny per se, but it *was* interesting. And despite the bullet holes in the kitchen and her wall of ovens, along with two that somehow had ricocheted inside the walk-in to hit the Freon line and cause the whole thing to have to be replaced, the holes had been filled, the stains cleaned up, and the front of house had gotten a facelift with new tables, paint, and a larger glass case.

All expenses she'd been planning on.

All expenses she'd been planning on in a *few* months.

But Dan had smoothed the way with the insurance company, and they were covering the replacement of the walk-in while the tab for the industrial cleanup of her kitchen was going to be covered by Dan's budget for the venture.

Which she was starting to suspect . . . okay, was beyond

suspecting and had moved into near certainty, that Dan and Laila didn't *actually* work for the federal government. For one, they seemed pretty free and lose with the rules—getting the insurance company to cover something they'd initially refused to, using their so-called federal dollars to clean her place up, the fancy private hospital, being able to install cameras and microphones that were absolutely undetectable, all in the span of a couple of days.

Molly thought that meant they had big bucks.

And she didn't think big bucks and a federal investigation mixed, especially with all of the budget cuts she'd been hearing about lately.

So yeah, she intended to press Dan for details, and use her instincts Laila had praised, to get to the bottom of the mystery.

And soon.

But right now, she was waiting for Jackson to wake up.

He'd slept through the night, through the checks on his wound, his blood pressure, his temperature with a scary sort of intensity . . . as in, he didn't groan or move or show any indication that someone was touching him. Instead, he just slept on, and it would have been seriously frightening if not for the fact that the nurses and doctor who checked on him were not concerned in the least.

But Molly didn't think she'd rest easy until he was back to feeling more like himself . . . and acting less like a Sleeping Beauty.

Knock-knock.

She glanced up and saw Laila was standing in the doorway.

"Can I come in?"

"Yes, of course." Molly closed her laptop with a sigh of relief. She'd been trying to weed through the spreadsheet Shannon had sent with the bakery's finances while attempting to appear as though she weren't counting every breath that Jackson took.

Laila had a bag from a fast food restaurant in one hand, a tray with two coffees in the other, and Molly wasn't going to lie, her stomach rumbled.

Yes, it was fast food.

Yes, she would have turned her nose up at it just the day before.

But today, coffee paired with an egg sandwich and greasy hash browns sounded just about perfect.

She reached for the bag then stopped when Laila held it against her chest.

"This isn't for you."

"O-oh." Molly's cheeks went hot. "I'm sorry. I thought—"

Laila grinned then held out the bag. "I'm just fucking with you. I'm guessing this is utter shit when compared to the stuff you make in your bakery." She set the tray on the small table next to the bed. "Wasn't sure how you take your coffee?"

"Just black," Molly told her. "I have enough sugar throughout the day."

Laila handed over a cup then proceeded to dump no less than six sugars and four little containers of cream into her own coffee. "What?" she said when Molly stared at her, eyebrows raised—because, seriously, Laila gave off tough, military badass vibes. She did not give off six sugars and four creamers vibes.

"Nothing," Molly said. "You do you."

Laila took a sip and sighed in pleasure. "I will. Also, let it be noted for the universe that I do not get enough sugar throughout the day, so I stock up on it first thing."

"Well, next time you're in the neighborhood, and when our little mafia problem is solved, come into the bakery, and I can provide you enough sugar to jumpstart your system for the day."

She nudged the other woman's shoulder. "I also promise that it'll be tastier than a fast food coffee and breakfast sandwich."

Laila snorted. "Twist my arm why don't you?" A beat. "You make croissants?"

"Chocolate-filled and traditional, every single day," Molly told her. "Flakey pastry, buttery layers—"

The egg sandwich was an inch from Laila's mouth, but at Molly's words she set it back down on the paper wrapper and frowned. "No fair, Ms. Baker."

"Hey, *I'm* the one promising you tasty treats."

"But you're not the one *with* tasty treats," Laila said. "So, eat your breakfast sandwich, drink your coffee, and tell me when exactly you're going to relax enough to sleep so that when this one"—she pointed at Jackson's still-sleeping form—"wakes up, he won't kill me or Dan for letting you run yourself into exhaustion."

"Um. That's not . . . " She trailed off when Laila's brow lifted.

Okay, so maybe she was counting breaths and freaking out about Jackson and the possibility of infection, or the chance of some stitch coming free and him bleeding out, or maybe that the surgeons had missed something—

"You don't have much of a poker face, do you?"

Molly sighed. "I'm guessing you don't need me to answer that."

Laila reached over and squeezed her hand. "I'm not going to tell you to stop worrying," she said. "But I'll just tell you that it'll get better."

"I'm guessing you're speaking from experience?"

A nod. "My line of work is not an easy one at times."

"I could see that," Molly said then asked softly, "And the nightmares? Do they ever really go away?"

Jackson shifted slightly in the bed, drawing her gaze before Laila could answer, her shoulders tensing as she waited to see if he would finally wake. When his eyelids fluttered and slid open, Laila stood, grabbing her food and drink. "Looks like that one is going to give you some peace of mind." She nodded at the untouched sandwich on the table. "Just make sure you *finally* eat something."

"Molly?" Jackson's voice was groggy.

Laila smiled, headed for the door. "For the record, the nightmares *do* go away. Over time they tend to fade on their own," she said. *"Though*, I have found t' having someone to hold you while you sleep makes that r by a little faster." A beat, a smile curving the corne mouth. "Lucky you, I think you have a volunteer." pause. "It also helps to actually *eat something.*"

Then she was gone, an used back on Jackson.

His chocolate eyes w and hot.

"Nightmares?" he a

"Um—"

He cut her off before could answer, asking, *"Actually* eat something?"

"Uh—"

Jackson's gaze flicked to the nightstand and he leaned up enough to grab the sandwich Laila had brought then shoved it into Molly's hands. "Food," he growled. "Then sleep."

"Jack—"

"Food."

"Are you trying to be a caveman?" she snapped. "Because it's not attractive."

His expression went thunderous. "Your skin is pale, those circles under your eyes are darker than that black coffee you like to drink, and your hands are shaking," he said. "You need to eat and rest."

Molly's eyes flicked down, saw that her hands were indeed trembling.

"*You're* telling *me* to rest."

His eyes narrowed. "Eat the fucking sandwich before you pass out, Molly."

Her temper flared, but also . . . she found she couldn't argue further with the man who'd taken a bullet for her, who'd been rushed into emergency surgery, who'd slept the last eighteen hours, and had done it hard, after declaring his love for her because his body needed healing.

She picked up the damn breakfast sandwich and started choking it down.

Yes, she was being dramatic and a fancy bitch about the fact it was from a fast food restaurant. It wasn't *that* bad—so the bread and egg and cheese wasn't her chocolate croissants or apple turnovers, but it was warm and food and filled her belly.

Add in some much-needed coffee, and she was feeling much better by the time she finished it.

"Happy?" she asked, setting the cup down on the table. "I ate—*oof!*"

One minute she was straightening from putting the coffee down, the next she was yanked forward, sprawling on the bed, instantly trying to get up, to move away from Jackson, lest she hurt him.

"Stop squirming," he ordered then huffed out a pained breath.

Molly immediately froze. "What the hell are you doing?" she whispered.

"Getting you to rest," he whispered back.

"I can't rest *here*," she said, still whispering.

"Nightmares," he replied softly, as though that were an explanation that made any sense. "Also, why are we whispering?"

"I don't know," she whispered then forced her voice back to normal. "Jackson, you had surgery yesterday, and you have a wound that's just barely begun to heal. You need space to do that."

"How am I supposed to rest if the woman I love isn't eating or sleeping?" he asked. "   uation were reversed, would you be able to just go bac   ?"

Well, put it that way

He touched her ch   expression telling her that he knew he'd won this rou

"Glad you're going   son." He tapped her lightly on the nose.

She narrowed her   n.

Jackson grinned. "   t I find it incredibly sexy when you glare at me?"

"That's not supposed to be the result of my glare," she muttered. "I still think I should move back to the chair. It reclines enough for me to lay down and—"

A finger to her lips. "Let me do this for you, love," he murmured. "I can't do much else, can't make this problem go away, can't suddenly manifest superhero powers and whisk you off to somewhere safe. But I *can* hold you if the nightmares come."

And how could she disagree with that?

"I'm not hurting you?"

"Having you in my arms feels nothing short of right."

Carefully, she shifted to her side, making sure to not put any part of her body near his wound, near the IV that was still pumping him full of saline and antibiotics. After a moment, he ignored her minute, tentative movements and just closed his arms around her, tugged her against his chest, and ordered, "Sleep."

Because it felt right to be held by him, because he sounded

drowsy himself, Molly didn't fight the order or bother to comment on his caveman-like tactics.

Instead, she closed her eyes and for the first time in days, fell asleep without a deluge of worry downpouring through her dreams.

TWENTY

Jackson

BEING SHOT SUCKED.

Just in case anyone was wondering.

He'd spent the last week hunkered down in the hospital trying to pretend that his injury was no big deal, all while feeling pathetically weak when his legs shook as they carried him to the toilet.

Because his first conscious action after making sure that Molly had gotten some food into her, as well as some rest, had been to get the fucking catheter out.

Going to the bathroom on his own seemed a necessary skill.

First, peeing on his own.

Second, making sure they were safe.

Also second, building on what he and Molly had started.

And third, world domination . . . *bahaha!*

He rolled his eyes at himself, knowing he couldn't blame the pain medication any longer for the horrible joke. Nope. That was all him and his stir-crazy brain.

Seven days confined to a bed, with only a few short breaks

and halting traipses down the private hospital's hallways to continue building his strength. Seven days where Molly had taken care of *everything* from managing to get into his laptop to get in touch with his assistant—he'd discovered that on the second day in bed, after sleeping for the majority of those two days, that he'd apparently developed appendicitis and was recovering. So, aside from a few calls to his CFO and COO, handing over the big projects, and an inbox that could never quite get to zero, Jackson didn't have much to do.

No meetings.

Nothing needing his approval.

Lots of sitting around, twiddling his thumbs, and watching some bad reality television show Laila, leader of the second team Dan had called in, had put on TV, and although he'd never admit it, Jackson was starting to see the appeal.

Molly, meanwhile, had not.

She wasn't used to time away from the bakery, wasn't used to not being on her feet all day, creating delicious masterpieces from flour and eggs and butter.

She had taken stir crazy and raised it one delivery of supplies to the hospital's kitchen, seven batches of different muffins, two of croissants, and one of apple turnovers.

Dan and Laila and their respective team members taking a turn at the hospital had been thrilled.

Jackson had kept his mouth shut.

Because the IV had come out shortly after the catheter and because that day he'd finally managed the strength to hobble down to the kitchen and check on her . . . and had gotten some treats for his trouble.

Plus, between the baking and the managing of her business, she didn't fight him on sleeping in his arms every night.

Slow and steady, rebuilding that trust, getting to hold her close, to smell her, to feel her against him. To admit that, he too, had nightmares and when she was next to him, he slept better because he knew she was safe.

But by tomorrow, he'd at least be allowed to return to the condo—now retrofitted with more security and additional body-guards. Dan's team was apparently tracking down a final few leads before they took action. "If we cast the net wide enough," he'd said, "we might finally be able to put this thing to an end once and for all."

An end once and for all sounded good.

Jackson was done with looking over his shoulder. He was finally ready to live his life.

With Molly.

Who breathed out a long-suffering sigh when the older female on screen lamented about the man she was supposed to be marrying—all without having ever seen him—and their seven-year age difference.

Again.

"I can't take this any longer."

She pushed up from her chair, nodding at Laila who was currently on watch and was somehow giving the impression of both devouring the train wreck on the television while also being aware of everything around her.

Case in point, she was on her feet, positioning herself between them and the door several seconds before the knock came at the door.

"Identify," she called.

This didn't worry Jackson because it was something that had happened the entire time he'd been awake to witness it. This time, like all the others, they heard a familiar voice rattle off a string of numbers and letters, which had Laila relaxing and the door opening after she said, "Cleared."

Dan poked his head in. "Hey," he announced. "I'm here to rescue you from reality TV."

Molly sighed in relief, Laila made a noise of protest, and Jackson stifled his response that it wasn't really saving if he wanted to know where the TV show was going.

Regardless, Mol saved him from blurting that out by announcing, "I'm going to bake."

"I'll walk with you," Laila said. "Suddenly too much testosterone in this room." She grabbed her stuff as Molly bent and brushed her lips across his, murmuring, "I'll be back in a little bit. Going to finish making those pumpkin muffins."

He watched them leave, mind prickling.

Maybe it was the testosterone comment from Laila, having learned over the week that the woman had spent most of her life surrounded by males and was certainly no stranger to rooms filled with testosterone—and that *those* rooms most definitely didn't have trashy reality TV shows blaring in their backgrounds.

Or maybe it was the pumpkin muffins.

Because Molly had told him she'd finished the batch that morning.

Unfortunately, by the time those two oddities punctuated his brain, by the time he mentioned them to Dan, and by the time they both tried to reach Molly and Laila, respectively, it was too late.

They were gone.

TWENTY-ONE

Molly

"WHAT IS IT?" she asked the moment they were out of earshot of the room, heading down the hall toward the stairwell that led to the kitchens.

"Wait." Laila tugged open the door, started heading down the stairs, with Molly following. They stopped about halfway down, Laila's gaze going above and below them, silently searching for long seconds until her eyes returned back to Molly's.

"It's tomorrow," she said. "They're going to make their move in the morning when we head to the condo."

Molly's breath caught. Shit. That sounded ominous. "So, we're not going to go? And why aren't we discussing this with Dan and Jackson?" she asked. "Shouldn't they know that—"

Laila reached out and squeezed her shoulder. "I'm worried that Dan might be in on it."

"What?" Molly's mouth fell open. "No." She shook her head. "That can't be right. He's been trying to solve this for four years. He's—"

"There's someone on the inside," Laila interrupted.

"I was right?" she asked carefully.

Laila nodded, releasing her arm. "I intercepted a coded message, encrypted on our server in a language that is supposed to be strictly for us—" A door opened above them, footsteps coming down. Laila tensed, her body between the person's and Molly's but when Laila saw who it was, she relaxed and stepped to the side.

It was a male agent Molly hadn't seen around before.

"Daniel," Laila said when he hesitated before moving by them. "Have you met Molly yet?"

"No." He stuck out his hand, and Molly shook it, intimidated by the sheer size of him. This was a man who could crush her like a toothpick. "Hi, I'm Daniel. Also known as the bigger, *smarter* Dan."

Laila grinned. "Who goes by *Daniel* because two Dans in the group is two too many."

"Rude." He winked. "Actually, I go by Daniel because it's more sophisticated."

"Also, he lost the game of rock-paper-scissors."

"A *tournament* of rock-paper-scissors."

"To-may-to, to-mah-to," Laila said. "Daniel and I go way back. Stitches come out?"

He nodded. "All recovered."

"Glad to hear it. I missed your dumb ass," Laila said, grinning to soften the insult, though Daniel didn't seem the least bit perturbed by it. "You heading out back?" she asked.

Another nod. "Yup. I'm on watch while Ryker gets some shuteye." He glanced at Molly, smiled. "Nice to meet you."

"You, too." She inwardly frowned, trying to understand why her brain was pinging, but then Laila turned and pushed through the door into the kitchen, studying the space for several long moments before waving Molly in then closing and leaning back against the door.

"I need you to be careful," Laila said. "The reason we're not up in that hospital room telling this to Dan and Jackson is because the message I intercepted was in Dan's code."

Molly gasped.

"I don't know if the person on the inside is really him, or if it's someone else who's trying frame him," Laila told her. "All I know is that this whole situation smells like high heaven, so I need you to stick close to Jackson, to me, and most of all to be careful."

She nodded. "I can do that."

Laila squeezed her arm.

"Good."

"You're not with the FBI or the CIA, are you?"

"If I told you that then I'd have to kill you."

Molly laughed.

Laila didn't.

In fact, her face might as well have been made of granite. Her blue eyes cold and unfathomable, her jaw tight, her shoulders rigid. She reached into her pocket and pulled out her cell phone.

Oh shit.

"Never mind," Molly said. "So . . . um . . . I'll just start mixing batter?"

Yes, the last was a question. No, she hadn't necessarily underestimated Laila, the other woman was clearly capable and strong. It was just that with all the reality TV and joking around, she'd sort of forgotten that the other woman was dangerous.

Okay, so she *had* underestimated Laila.

She wouldn't be making that mistake again.

Her eyes darted to the door, mentally calculating her chances of getting by Laila if *she* turned out to be the mole.

Maybe she could put her sheet pan skills to the test?

But just as she'd started to inch toward the stack of them near the oven, Laila grinned and bent over laughing. "I'm just fucking with you."

Molly didn't find that nearly as amusing. "That's not funny."

Laila was still laughing as she straightened. "It is to me." She threw an arm around Molly's shoulders. "But seriously, all I can tell you is that I work for an entity that has a particular interest in making the world a better place."

"Does this entity fund this hospital?"

"Sometimes the work is dangerous and certain accommodations need to be made."

"How wonderfully vague," Molly deadpanned.

A flash of white teeth. "We're good at vague. But we're also good at keeping people safe." She rolled her eyes. "Or usually, anyway," she muttered. "When we don't have someone on the inside working against us." She dropped her arm, reached for the door. "Okay, so let's skip making the pumpkin muffins and get you glued to Jackson's side, so I can kick some ass and figure out—"

Laila didn't get to finish the sentence.

A puff of air blew past Molly's ear, and as she whipped around to see it, she heard Laila grunt, heard the soft, "*Fuck. Run, Molly.*"

Then it was too late.

Another puff of air.

A sharp pain in her stomach.

She glanced down, and there was a bright red dart sticking out of her abdomen. Then she looked up, saw the hulking

Maksim, who'd been waiting outside the elevator at Jackson's condo.

He didn't wait this time.

He came toward her.

And the last thing she saw before her brain went fuzzy and her legs weak, were his huge, beefy hands reaching for her.

Then the world went black.

TWENTY-TWO

Jackson

THE CALL CAME after Dan and his team members had torn the hospital apart, not finding a single sign of Molly and Laila, aside from Laila's cell phone, unlocked, an emergency code on the keypad, but not sent.

One agent, Daniel, said he'd seen them as they'd headed for the kitchen, when he'd been on his way to the back of the hospital for a guard change. But by the time the agent he'd been relieving had made his way back inside, they been gone. The phone the only clue that something was wrong.

Jackson had long given up the hospital gown, had forced his ass out of bed to help search as much as Dan would let him.

But he hadn't turned down the chair Dan had offered *after* he'd helped.

And now, Jackson's cell was ringing.

He glanced at Dan, who looked to the agent next to him with furious dark eyes and an expression that said he was going to kill whoever was responsible. "Ready for the trace?" The man nodded. "Okay," Dan said turning back to Jackson. "Answer, but on speaker."

Jackson swiped his finger across the screen, hit speakerphone. "Hello?"

A voice heavy with a Russian accent said, "Point Bonita Lighthouse. Midnight. Bring the hard drives currently in KTS's possession."

"Where are Molly and Laila?" he asked. "I need to hear that they're—"

Click.

"Fuck," he muttered, tos   phone onto the desk. "Fucking hell."

"It's clearly trap," the pis   n at Dan's side spat.

"Yeah, Ryker," Dan said   ' He glanced at his watch. "But we have three hours. '   .o get the drives here, so we have something to negotiaᵗ   )aniel?" He turned, nodded at the other agent. "Can   headquarters? Tell them that we need some leeway." J   d at Jackson. "If you work fast, can you make them loo'   program? Something that looks real enough that we can hand over for the switch? If we use dummy drives to get Molly and Laila out—"

Look, Jackson got it.

He'd been staying mostly to the sidelines for the majority of this investigation, letting the agents lead the way since that was their expertise.

But this?

No. No more.

"Absolutely fucking *not*," he snapped. "I'm not putting the woman I love at risk just because some politician with something to hide might get outed from my program. I've sat back for too long, letting you guys drive this, but I'm done." He shoved to his feet. "They can *have* the fucking program, can use it to glean whatever fucking personal information—porn habits, racist comments, search habits—they want. I don't give a shit any longer." He slapped his hands on the desk. "Because I'm done risking Molly's life for this. I'm done risking my own life and everyone else's. Is it the most noble thing in the world to turn it over? *No.* But *no l*￼ ￼ will I give up everything important to me for a program ￼ one else is going to make in a few years anyway."

Dan stared a￼ ￼ intense pools of deep blue.

Then he tu￼ ￼odded at Daniel. "Make the call. Get the drives here

Daniel no￼ ￼eft.

Dan wai￼ ￼e door shut then came over and clapped Jackson on ￼ ￼er. "I promise that you're done having to give things ￼ ￼t. "Nice speech by the way."

Then before Jackson could ask Dan what in the fuck he meant by that, the agent began talking.

And suddenly, a hell of a lot more pieces fell into place.

Less than an hour later, the drives were in the back of an SUV, Jackson was sandwiched by a pair of muscled military guys, and they were heading to the lighthouse at Point Bonita.

This time he wasn't going to sacrifice to get Molly back.

He was going to fight for her.

Until his last breath.

TWENTY-THREE

Molly

SHE WOKE to someone nudging her hard in the side.

To someone hissing in her ear.

"Molly! Wake up, now!"

Boulders were attached to her eyelids, but she managed to wrench them open, to see that she and Laila were . . . *somewhere.*

She sniffed and inhaled salt. Looked around and saw trees and dirt and darkness barely punctuated by moonlight. Listened and could hear waves crashing at a distance.

Were they near the ocean?

"*Molly.*"

She blinked, focused on the someone in front of her. On *Laila* in front of her, arms bound, eye swelling, and normally contained blond ponytail scattered to hell and back.

"Laila," she whispered, instinctively keeping her voice low in volume to match the other woman's. "Where are we?"

A shake of her head. "No time. The guards have finally gone. I need out of these restraints."

Molly glanced at the zip ties that were wrapped around Laila's wrists, her arms pulled tightly behind her back. Her own wrists were free, but that probably had more to do with her not posing a threat.

Too bad there weren't any sheet pans around.

"Is there a trick to getting them off?" she asked quietly.

"Yeah," Laila said, her teeth flashing in the dim light. "A knife."

Molly shifted to her knees. "Well, I don't happen to have one of those."

Another flash of white teeth. "Well, I *do*. Reach into my bra, but carefully. There's one sewn into the band."

"Sewn in?"

"You never know when it might come in handy." Laila gave a small shrug. "And it's usually missed because the people searching are too focused on other things. Here," she added when Molly didn't move, just stared at her incredulously. "Under my shirt on this side."

"Got it," Molly said.

"Be careful," Laila told her, "I can feel that it's come loose of the sheath."

Nodding, she put her hands under the T-shirt and moving up to the band of Laila's bra then sliding between the fabric and her skin, trying to find the knife without stabbing herself or feeling Laila up.

She didn't succeed on either effort.

"Ouch!" she muttered, feeling the tip dig into her finger then carefully shifting back and working at the other end. "How are you able to move without stabbing yourself?"

"Lots of practice," Laila quipped. "Though usually it stays in the sheath."

"I'm guessing there aren't a lot of females in your can't-tell-you-without-killing-you entity," she said, running her finger carefully along the edge of the knife.

"Not so much."

"Well, tell whoever it is that designed this thing to go back to the drawing board," she muttered. "This could kill you."

"In fairness, I'm not usually in this particular position when I'm trying to retrieve it."

"*In fairness,* I don't think they're all that familiar with the inner workings of the female bra."

Laila snorted. "I think they're probably more familiar than either of us."

Molly froze then thought of the muscled badasses she'd seen over the last week, "Okay, fine. You're probably right."

"What a sad thing to be right about."

Molly snorted then, "Got it!" She tugged at the handle, feeling it come loose of whatever string or casing it had gotten stuck on. "I keep thinking someone is going to step out of the trees and call 'Cut!' at any time," she said, carefully sliding the blade from beneath Laila's bra and T-shirt. "Then ask me to do it again, only with more fondling."

"Not sure that's possible," Laila said.

"Hilarious." She held up the blade, thin and slender, but also scarily sharp, as her bleeding finger could attest. "How should I do this?" Last thing she wanted was to cut Laila.

"Just slip it in and tug," Laila said.

Molly blurted, "That's what he said."

Then froze and her gaze met Laila's, smiles breaking out on their faces. "I didn't think I'd be the type of person who'd be making jokes when I'm about to die," Molly said, shifting around and doing as Laila instructed—shoving the blade in the gap and yanking it toward her. It took a surprising amount of force to cut through the tie, and she suspected Laila's wrists didn't come out of the endeavor unscathed.

She didn't complain though, didn't do anything other than spin, take the knife from Molly's hands, and say, "You're not going to die. That's the first thing you need to remember. Second," she said. "Laughter is a way to cope with stressful situations. Keep it so you can freak out later instead of now."

Molly nodded, sucked in a breath. "Okay. Pretend to be a badass now. Cry later."

A punch to her shoulder. "Exactly." Laila shimmied and pulled the knife's sheath from her bra, covered the blade, and then stuck it in the back of her pants. "Ready?" she asked.

"For what?" Molly was blinking, stunned at how fast Laila had moved.

"For your first lesson in badassery."

And then she showed Molly how to launch herself over the cliff.

TWENTY-FOUR

Jackson

"DOESN'T MAKE ANY SENSE," Daniel muttered as they all piled out of the SUV. "Why would they knowingly corner themselves?"

They had pulled into the parking lot, and the lighthouse was a short hike ahead of them.

A short *dead-end* hike.

"Because they're not planning on being cornered," Ryker muttered. "It's a trap, dude."

"Yeah," Dan agreed, checking the straps on his backpack. "They want the drives. The rest of us are collateral." He glanced at Jackson. "You sure you're up for this?"

"Yup." Jackson adjusted the bulletproof vest he wore, the one he was all too aware didn't protect his head in the least, and tried to summon up some of the same confidence these guys had when he didn't have a gun . . . not that *having* a gun would mean anything, since he had no clue how to use one.

But he digressed.

Because they had a half-mile hike ahead of them, one that

would be easy on a normal day, but one that seemed daunting in the dark, especially when he was recovering from a bullet wound.

Jackson didn't say any of that.

Instead, when Dan said, "Fifteen minutes. Let hit it," he followed the other man who followed Daniel, and was trailed by Ryker.

Quiet.

It was very quiet as they walked.

Well, *they* were quiet, not making any noise as they moved, not the crunching of rocks or a stick being broken beneath their boots, not a muttered curse as they tripped over a bump in the path.

Nope. All the noise came from Jackson.

And knowing that, he tried to walk carefully and silently . . . but he just didn't have the skill.

He was also slowing them down, not just because of his injury but because these men could move.

Post-bullet Jackson wasn't currently in the best shape of his life.

But then, his ineptitudes turned out to be a good thing. Because the path narrowed and turned a corner, a metal bridge seeming to spring up out of nowhere as it spanned a huge gulf below them.

Shouting erupted. Shouting in *Russian*.

Flashlights flicked on, bouncing through the dark in the distance and then closer.

Footsteps pounded along the metal bridge.

Before Jackson could open his mouth to ask what they should do, he was yanked back and to the side, Ryker moving in front of him. "Down," he hissed, and Jackson didn't hesitate, didn't question the order. He hit the dirt, wincing when his stitches protested. "Stay," Ryker snapped.

Jackson stayed.

The footsteps pounded closer then closer then . . . Dan made a gesture with his hand and Daniel *moved*. He grabbed the first man that came over the bridge, wrestling him to the ground while Dan took the next, and then Ryker took the third. They were silent, the three men between him and the mafia as they silently immobilized the figures sprinting over the bridge.

Then he felt something hit his shoulder. Hard.

But not where the guys were focused. Not in front of them.

It came from *beneath* them.

He twisted, felt his eyes go wide, and had to bite back a curse. Because beneath the bridge, clinging to the edge of the craggy cliffside were Molly and Laila, the latter with a knife clutched between her teeth.

Jackson didn't think.

He moved, shimmying forward and reaching over the edge. He grabbed Molly's arm, the back of her pants, and yanked her up next to him on level ground, but when he turned to help Laila, he saw she was already up, hustling toward the group of men, joining the fray with a sharp word to Dan.

Ryker froze for a heartbeat, his hands around the neck of one of the men who'd come over the bridge, then he moved, tearing a gun out of another one's hands, as Laila slipped between them.

The *pop-pop* of silenced gunfire.

Flashlights shining, blinding him for long moments before his eyes adjusted again.

Scuffling on the path.

The sound of fists meeting flesh.

But the entire fight was quieter than he would have expected, certainly quieter than a fight scene in any action movie he'd ever watched.

And then it was over.

A line of bodies on the ground. Laila, Ryker, Daniel, and Dan standing over them.

"Any more?" Dan asked Laila.

"Not sure," she said. "Unconscious until ten minutes ago."

"You climbed a fucking cliffside when you were unconscious?" Ryker snapped.

Laila rolled her eyes. "I know you'll reconsider the logic of your words later," she muttered. "For now—"

If Jackson never saw another circular, red light for the rest of his life, it would be too soon. But this dot wasn't on Laila or Molly or Daniel or even on Ryker. It was on Dan, squarely in the center of his chest.

He glanced down, cursed.

Footsteps coming over the bridge. The light drifting up from the bulletproof vest, centering on Dan's forehead as Maksim emerged from the shadows. He stopped out of reach and his gaze slipped from Dan and the group of agents, over to Jackson, who tucked Molly behind him.

"I'll take the hard drives now."

He knew.

Maksim somehow knew that none of the badasses had the drives. He knew they were in the backpack that Jackson was carrying.

"Why do you want the hard drives so badly?" Laila asked, attempting to draw his attention, but Maksim didn't shift his focus from Jackson . . . or move his gun from Dan's head.

"How fast can you duck, Agent Plantain?"

Dan's spine went stiff.

"Also," Maksim said. "I don't give a shit about the program that fucking pain in the ass made." His word hardened. "I want those fucking hard drives."

"What's on them that's so important?" Laila asked.

Maksim smiled, but it wasn't a happy smile. This was laced

with cruelty, anger, and . . . satisfaction. His eyes flicked between the agents. "Well, aside from it having information that is critical to Alexei's innocence—"

"Read: there is blackmail material on someone in Spain that will get him out," Laila muttered.

Maksim's expression shifted, more satisfaction creeping in. "I think that is what you Americans would call splitting hairs." He shifted his gun, moving it from Dan over to Molly. "I was going to only wound her before," he said to Jackson. "Just to *motivate* you to come to the right conclusion and hand over what our money bought."

"I returned the investment," Jackson said. "Once I figured out what you wanted, I gave it all back."

"But you couldn't return the investment of our time." He sighed, shaking his head. "You Americans always want and want, but never are willing to give. Although, perhaps that isn't fair. I have found one individual here who is—"

Daniel was going to move.

Jackson didn't stop to process how he knew that. Instead, he watched in horror.

Daniel yanked Laila's knife from her hand and threw it. The blade flew through the air and . . . struck home, cutting off Maksim mid-sentence. His body crumpled, collapsing to the metal frame of the bridge.

"What the fuck was that?" Dan spun, grabbing Daniel's vest and shaking him violently. "We had him. We fucking *had* him—"

Laila got in his face, followed by Ryker, and the conversation got heated.

Daniel shoved them away, turned to Jackson. "Give them to me," he snapped. "Now."

"Daniel." Laila's tone was devastated. "*No.*"

But the man who had stopped just a few feet away, didn't

react, didn't seem to care that while her knife was in Maksim's chest, Daniel might as well have stabbed it directly into Laila's heart. "Hand it over."

Jackson felt a tug on the backpack and let his shoulders relax, his arms to fall so that Molly could slip it free. Fine. Daniel could have it.

If it meant they would all be safe then—

Molly stepped to the side, holding the backpack, and drawing Daniel's focus. He took a step toward them, hand extended, and . . . Molly launched the backpack over the cliff.

"*No*—"

The sentence cut off abruptly as Daniel was momentarily detained by Ryker, but then he was free and he was running— not toward the parking lot, but over the bridge.

His footsteps clambered across the metal, followed by Dan, Ryker, and Laila's as they gave chase.

But Jackson couldn't focus on that, couldn't take more time to think, to process the roar of a boat's motor as it came to life and then faded away. Instead, he just needed to feel and react and live without walls between him and the rest of the world. He spun, took Molly into his arms, and hugged her tightly.

"It's over," Dan said, when he came back, Daniel conspicuously absent. "For you, it's finally over."

And for the first time in four years, Jackson knew that when the other man said those words, it was the truth.

Just as he believed Dan when he added, Laila and Ryker coming up behind them, "For us, this is just beginning."

TWENTY-FIVE

Molly, A Week Later

"HOW ARE we just ꭎ   to go back to real life when we've spent the last coɩ   ꭍeeks playing commando?" she asked Jackson, stepping   his legs as he sat in "his" stool in the bakery's kitchen.

"Easy," he said, sliɩ   arms around her. "Because we weren't *actually* the coɩ   ꞌꞌ

She wrinkled her nose. "ʙut, I *did* climb a cliff in the dark of night, after being drugged with a poison dart—"

"Don't remind me." Jackson shuddered.

"I also finally got to put my sheet pan throwing skills to good use."

He grinned. "True. Who would have thought that all those years of throwing things at my head would be useful?"

Molly laughed, leaning against his chest. "I love you, baby."

"I love you, too." He touched her cheek. "But when I think what could have happened . . . Promise me, no more cliff climbing, no more playing at being a commando. I don't think my heart can take it."

As if she was suddenly going to go to badass school. She had rolls to bake, muffins to perfect. "I promise," she said. "Any more cliff climbing will be in a perfectly controlled environment. With ropes and a safety net and—"

He kissed her. "No climbing."

She kissed him. "No more arguing."

"What's the fun in that?"

He had a point. Which was why she nipped his bottom lip and said, "I think I may take up target practice . . ."

Jackson growled and tugged her close, tickling her lightly on the ribs, which turned into tickling a different body part that she very much enjoyed. Still, it was the middle of the day and they both had work they should be doing, so she kissed him lightly on the lips then straightened. "I know something that *my* heart can take."

He nuzzled her throat. "What's that?"

"You taking me on a first date—" She stopped, and shook her head. "Or another first date . . . a *second* first date?"

Jackson grinned, brushed her hair out of her face. "What if I already said I had it planned?"

"I'd ask if it includes chocolate and alcohol."

"As a matter of fact . . ."

"Mmm." She nipped his jaw. "Well, then I'd say I accept."

"Friday," he told her. "When you don't have to be up so early and can sleep in the next day."

Molly's heart swelled, because aside from the whole Jackson-nearly-dying and the her-being-kidnapped thing . . . these last few weeks had been something special. Because he had let the walls down, because he learned and paid attention to the little things—her schedule—and the big things—how she was in love with him but wanted to have the time to get to know him again, for them to learn each other. Because they deserved to take the time, they deserved the space and ability and even the lovely fluttering feeling that came from building a strong foundation between them.

Even if it heavily featured a crumbling cliffside in the First Act.

Or Second Act. Or maybe it had been during the finale?

The point was . . . this was their chance, whether it be the start of the sequel, or just the lovely paved road that led to their happily ever after.

And know what the awesome thing about sequels was?

That sometimes they began with a plot twist.

Which was why she tugged Jackson off the stool, took him by the hand and led him to her office. The cameras had been removed. The microphones were gone. The bakery was closed, her employees long gone as she'd gotten ahead on the following day's baking while he caught up on his emails.

"What are you doing?" he asked.

She closed t pushed him back against it. "Well, funny story. I did rch about gunshot wounds . . ." She let her hand drift est, coasting over the waistband of his slacks, dipping rns out that while sex is still off the table"—she dropp nees—"blow jobs aren't."

"Mol—"

He groaned when s im. "Consider this you getting lucky before the first dat

Then before he coulc ther, she closed her lips over his cock, sucked him deep, violly showed him how lucky he was about to get.

And when she finished, coaxing him through to the other side, Jackson nudged her back onto the desk, dropped to his knees, and *then* he showed her exactly how lucky she already was.

But then again, she already knew that.

EPILOGUE

PART ONE

Jackson, One Year Later

THE WHITE DRESS.

The flower arrangements.

The glittering diamond ring.

They had absolutely none of that.

Instead, they had croissants and apple turnovers. They had a minister standing in the front of bakery's display case. They had Molly's patrons as witnesses.

The only thing that was frilly and white was the apron Molly wore courtesy of her friend, Shannon.

But right now, he needed to pull the woman he loved away from the *thing* she loved most in the world . . . or perhaps, the second most. Well, frankly, he wasn't sure where he fell on the scale some days, certainly not when she was talked so sweetly to her rolls as she shaped them or her dough as it rose.

First or second, that was fine with him.

Because Jackson knew that at the end of the day, Molly came home to him and the rolls, they stayed at the—okay, sometimes they came home, too.

And that was fine.

What was not fine, however, was the sight of his woman, the one he was waiting to marry in the other room, crying.

He rushed over. "Baby, what's wrong?"

"I can't do this," she said. "I-I just can't—"

His heart sank. His stomach twisted itself into knots. His first instinct was to tell her that they didn't have to go through with this, that they could give themselves more time, that he'd step back and let her get her head together.

But . . . fuck that.

He was done with *that*. Done with stepping back and not fighting for the things he wanted.

Jackson had Molly back in   nd this last year had been, hands down, the best or   ife. So, no, he wasn't going to step back or send his   on her merry way. He loved her, wanted her as his   his partner, as his best friend.

"I'm going to marry you   t, and, yes, his tone was sharp. But when Molly's ey   to his, surprise lifting her brows, he kept talking. "No   have to get married today, if it feels too soon. No, we   e to get married next week or even next year. But I love you, Mol. You're *it* for me." He brushed a finger under each eye, wiping away the tears. "So, you *are* going to marry me, you *are* going to keep building our life together with me, and you *are*—"

She kissed him.

Long and wet and hot, and when she finally pulled back, his lungs burned, desperate for oxygen.

But before he could suck in enough air to regain his voice, Molly spoke. Thus, further proving how much more of a badass she was than him. Cliff-climbing, minimal need for oxygen, crafting deliciousness from flour, sugar, and butter that had taken the whole city by storm, no big deal.

"You silly man," she murmured, lips close enough that they brushed his when he spoke. "I wasn't talking about marrying you."

He frowned. "Then what?"

She backed up, shifting to the side, and Jackson noticed what was on the table. "*This.*"

"What is it?" he asked, staring at the blackened circles sitting on the counter.

Molly's cheeks went red. "Our wedding cake."

"I thought you didn't want to bother with a cake," he said, cautiously poking a finger into the pan, into what once had resembled cake, and now resembled a brick.

"I didn't," she said, flush spreading fuller. "But *you* did."

That was true.

He might not have given a shit about the dress or the church or even writing their sentimental vows.

But *he* cared about the cake.

Stupid.

And still, he'd always imagined his wedding punctuated with a cake, cutting it with their hands laced together over the knife, then messily feeding Molly a morsel, kissing off a dollop of buttercream frosting from her nose. It was the one thing he'd been able to picture with crystal clarity from the beginning.

Chocolate cake. White frosting.

That was it.

A small thing in the grand scheme of things, but he had also wanted Molly to have something sweet that she didn't have to make herself. So he'd offered to order one from a different bakery.

She'd flipped. He'd let it drop.

And she'd made him a cake anyway.

His lips began curving up.

Well, *burned* it.

"Honey."

She wrinkled her nose. "I blame it on the bullet holes in the oven."

"I thought the oven was replaced."

"Shh." A shake of her head. "We're ignoring that detail. It was the bullets. Most definitely. They must have made the timer malfunction."

Jackson tugged her against his chest. "Nice try, baby." He bent and nipped at her lips. "What was it really?"

Her expression softened, but she didn't argue or defer further. "I got distracted."

"You?" He lifted a brow. "When baking?"

A shrug. "It happens to the best of us."

"But not to *you*." Shifting, he brushed his lips over her cheek, dragged them down he ʰroat, nipping at the spot just above her collarbone that neve ɪ make her shiver.

"Not to me," she murmu ɪot usually anyway." She laced her hand through his. ʻ . ."

His stomach clenched. grown a lot over the last year, had gone to therapy, mitted to tearing down the walls and forcing the li nside of him to grow up. Because of that, he was a' without being too terrified of the answer, "Just what?"

"Just thinking abou ' she said, and took their joint hands, placed them on her apron covered stomach. "Because it turns out this is actually going to be a shotgun wedding."

Jackson felt his mouth drop open, but inside his heart soared.

"Really?"

She grinned, nodded. "*Really* really."

His eyes burned, but just as he'd done over the last year, he embraced the burn, the feelings, the intense emotions instead of boxing them up or keeping them out or running scared. Still, he wasn't exactly eloquent. "Mol," he murmured. "Baby, that's . . ."

Amazing. Wonderful. Unexpected. Frightening. The best fucking news of his life.

But she knew.

Knew that a   e thoughts were running through his head even thoug   ds might not be flowing through his lips. She knew.   n and his heart. Knew how much building a family   together meant for both of them.

Which was wl   ply lifted up on tiptoe, pressed her lips against his brie   ien took his hand, saying, "I know, Jackson. I know."

He stared into tl   ous green eyes for a long moment.

Then he straight   tugged her toward the front of the bakery. "Forget the c   ...ie to get married."

She didn't argue.

They said their I Do's, they kissed in front of a cheering group of customers, and then . . . Jackson kissed a dollop of apple turnover filling from Molly's nose.

For the record, it was every bit as tasty as buttercream frosting.

EPILOGUE

PART TWO

Kate

DISGUSTED, she walked out of the bakery.

Mostly with herself for being jealous over the clearly happy couple.

Although, partly because they were so ridiculously happy. Come *on*. Who looked into each other's eyes with such devotion and joy while getting married in a freaking bakery with mostly strangers looking on?

No dress or cake—counterintuitive as that sounded, considering they were getting married in a freaking bakery.

No flowers, which would be Kate's weakness because she loved gardening and arranging flowers, having spent most of her extra money on sprucing up her backyard.

The inside might be a disaster.

But the backyard was a lush, gorgeous retreat.

Not that it mattered because she didn't have anyone to share it with. Least of which a gorgeous hunk of a man who stared at her with love in his eyes and tenderness in his smile.

Yes, she was bitter.

So, it was the perfect time for her cell to ring, her mother on the line.

Deal with the torture now? Or wait until it frothed to full power later?

She was already cranky and jaded and in a bad mood, so she might as well deal with her loving, but very nosy and interfering mother now. No sense in wasting a good mood later.

Because there *would* be a later.

Her mother loved her, that was never in doubt. What could *possibly* be questioned was the amount of attention she gave to her children's lives.

Attention that was now squarely focused on Kate.

On the fact that she was single when her two younger siblings were happily married, and her younger sister had recently popped out a kid.

Impressive. Beautiful—which she knew because she'd been in the delivery room.

But also . . . not *her*.

Hence, the increase in motherly calling.

Sighing, Kate swiped a finger to the screen and put her phone to the screen. "Hey, Mom."

"I've got the perfect man for you to bring to the Christmas party. He's a doctor and . . ."

Her mother continued talking, expounding on all of the wonderfulness that was this doctor. The trouble was that Kate was done with being set up. Her family were great at finding their own soulmates, their own happily ever afters . . . unfortunately that same ability didn't extend to her.

Either *by* her or *for* her.

It never failed to end in disaster. Both for her *and* for her date.

So, as much as she longed to have a man who she could call her own, one who'd call her his in return . . . she was taking a break from dating, from men, and most definitely from being set up.

"Mom," she began. "I'm not actually—"

"He's a doctor, isn't bald, and can have a conversation about something other than himself, Katie," her mother said. "He is a catch."

Who would turn into the world's worst asshole when he was around her.

Because that was her superpower.

Transforming seemingly *wonderful* men in lying, cheating, arrogant, self-centered, mansplaining, assholes.

And being that lightning didn't tend to strike the same place multiple times, Kate had decided on a hiatus from the opposite sex. Some time to sort out what was happening inside of her to make everyone she dated turn into a jerk.

This wasn't about all men on the planet being the bad guys, or her always picking wrong, or even about her family trying to set her up with a bunch of douche canoes. There was something wrong inside of *her*, something intrinsically wrong with the way she interacted with the men in her life.

So, a break.

Time to figure her shit out.

It was just . . . Christmas.

All of her family in one place. The huge party with the whole neighborhood. Everyone paired off and happy and gathering under the mistletoe her mother hung in each and every doorway.

And her.

Alone.

The pitying gazes plentiful.

Or worse . . . the copious conversations where all the happy people constantly threw every single male with half a brain cell in Kate's direction.

My cousin is in town and fresh out of a relationship . . .

I have a coworker who's new to the area. He's looking for someone . . .

My ex-husband would be perfect for you—he's actually a great guy . . .

And more.

Kate just couldn't take it, couldn't stand the idea of another Christmas party at her parents' house matched with someone who didn't fit her, or worse spending the entire extravaganza alone and in the corner, playing wallflower.

She wanted excitement.

She wanted someone who could be unequivocally hers.

She wanted someone who saw inside her and didn't run off in a panic.

". . . and Katie, love, he's going to be at dinner this Friday so that you two can get to know each other better—"

Fucking hell.

Family dinner *and* the Christmas Extravaganza?

Please. God. *No.*

"Um, Mom—"

"Remember he's got all his hair—"

"Actually, Mom. I'm kind of seeing—"

"And his stomach doesn't hang over his belt—"

"That's not—I don't really care about that—"

"*And* he's got the loveliest blue—"

"I'm engaged!" she screamed, cutting off her mother's solil-oquy of all things doctor, and successfully drawing the attention of random strangers on the sidewalk. Which was a hard thing to do in San Francisco—because it was San Francisco and these streets had seen a lot of shit—but also could only further confirm that she'd screamed it like a complete and total lunatic.

Shrieking *I'm engaged* on street corners.

What every man wanted.

"Katie?" her mom asked. "Did you say you're engaged?"

No. No, she wasn't. Not even close. She was on a break from anyone with a Y chromosome, mostly to save them from herself.

But also . . . there was joy in her mom's tone.

Absolute joy that she had never heard directed at her. To her brother, when he'd announced he was proposing to Chelsea, then again at his wedding this last summer (during which Kate had fended off the worst setup of all setups, The Can't Take No For An Answer Setup). Her mother had expressed that joy when her sister had announced she was pregnant, and again after her adorable niece had been born.

But she'd *never* given it to Kate.

Which was probably the reason she let the crazy keep rolling along.

Why instead of saying, "No, Mom. You heard wrong," she said, "Yes, I am, and you'll get to meet him Friday at dinner."

Horror flowed through her as intensely as her mother's excitement poured through the airwaves, expressing her joy at meeting him, her joy at Kate having finally found a slice of her own happy.

"What's his name, honey?"

Oh fuck.

"What's that?" Kate asked, panic swarming to overtake horror. "You're breaking up."

Oh shit. Oh shit. She hadn't thought this through. She needed—

"I asked his name—"

"Hello?" More panic. More horror. More pretending the call was cutting out because she had to end this conversation now. Hell, she should have never picked up the call in the first place. "Mom? *Hello?*"

"Katie!"

Shit. Shit. *Shit.* "I can't hear you," she said. "If you can hear me. I'll call you later." She hung up.

Or never.

As in, she'd never call her family again. As in, she was moving to a deserted island and changing her name and—

Fuck.

Because despite all of the setups and the pity and the fact that they'd found their happy, she loved her family. So. Damned. Much. And she also loved that stupid fucking Christmas party, even when she was lonely.

"*Ugh.*" Kate groaned, feet sliding to a stop on that dirty San Franciscan sidewalk.

She had a choice here.

She also knew she wasn't going to make the right one.

Because, instead of calling her mother back and telling her she'd heard wrong, that she wasn't engaged, Kate opened Instagram, tapped on the profile of a man she'd been following for a while now, who'd followed her back and commented on a few of her posts, and . . . sent a message.

Later, she'd want to pretend she'd been drinking.

But in *that* moment, the only thing she was consumed with was desperation.

And lust. She couldn't deny lust was also her downfall.

Because surprisingly, shockingly, *insanely* the man from social media, the one whose abs had made her fall just a little in love with him . . .

He said yes.

And suddenly, Kate had a fiancé.

EPILOGUE

PART THREE

Dan

HE SLIPPED OUT of the bac   bakery, after having
watched Jackson and Molly final   eir way to the happy
ending they deserved.

No big church or puffy dress

Just two people who were in l

People who had almost misseu their chance because he
couldn't get his shit done.

"Fuck," he muttered, so damned tired of the guilt and yet
knowing that it was just part of the job. When he'd been cherry-
picked from the FBI a few years before and folded into the
private sector, Dan had already been well-familiar with the fail-
ures that were common in this line of work.

Not every case was solved.

Not everyone came out alive.

Not every ending was happy.

Dan got that. He . . . just hadn't expected to find it so
fucking depressing to be working for an agency with a bigger
reach, who took on bigger bad guys from around the world.

Because despite the larger budget, the greater access to resources. Sometimes the bad guys still won.

And the only thing he hated more than the bad guys winning was when that unhappiness or death or boulder hanging over someone's head he was supposed to be helping was *his* fault.

"I knew you'd be here."

Dan didn't react. He might feel like a failure when it came with taking down the Mikhailova clan, but he was damned good at being aware of his surroundings, of keeping himself alive.

So, he knew that Laila was there, had slipped out the back door of the bakery, having felt the same connection with Molly and Jackson, and wanting to see them happy.

Because happy didn't happen often enough in this industry.

But just as he knew Laila had emerged from inside, even though she'd hardly made a sound when opening that heavy metal door, Dan also knew that Ava had come out behind her.

Ava.

Peaches. Humid summer days. Whisky and lemonade and—

Fuck. *Ava.*

She strode over to him, curves in a compact body, shining brown hair swept up into a ponytail that swung behind her shoulders as she moved, strength and confidence . . . and so many painful memories.

Her eyes looked right through him, minimizing everything that had happened between them two years ago.

Then those eyes narrowed, focused on him, seared straight into his soul.

"We found the hard drives."

A beat as Laila came forward and crossed her arms, expression furious.

"And we know what's on them."

COMING SOON

Read Kate's story in Bad Engagement, coming October 12, 2020. Preorder your copy and www. books2read.com/BadEngagement.

―――――――

And don't miss Dan's story in a brand new series! Riding The Edge, book 1 in the KTS series is coming December 7, 2020. Preorder at www.books2read.com/RidingTheEdge

BILLIONAIRE'S CLUB

Bad Night Stand

Bad Breakup

Bad Husband

Bad Hookup

Bad Divorce

Bad Fiancé

Bad Boyfriend

Bad Blind Date

Bad Wedding

Bad Engagement

BILLIONAIRE'S CLUB

Did you miss any of the other Billionaire's Club books? Check out excerpts from the series below or find the full series at www.amazon.com/gp/product/B07JVRRGCT

———

Bad Night Stand
Book One
www.books2read.com/BadNightStand

Abby

"I'M THE BEST FRIEND," I said and lifted my chin, forcing my words to be matter-of-fact. I'd been through this before. "You might be fuckable to the nth degree and perfect for Seraphina, but I refuse to set her up with a liar."

In a movement too quick for my brain to process, my stool was shoved to the side and I was pinned against the bar, heavy hips pressing into me, a hard chest two inches from my mouth.

Seraphina whipped around at the movement and I could just see her over Jordan's shoulder, her blue eyes concerned.

"Hi, Seraphina, I'm Jordan," he said, calm as can be, gaze locked onto my face then my eyes when mine invariably couldn't stay away. "I'm going to borrow your friend for a minute."

"Abs?" she asked, and I knew she'd go to bat for me right then and there if I needed her to.

"Weasel or no?" I managed to gasp out. For some reason, I couldn't catch my breath.

Not that it had anything to do with Jordan.

No, it had *everything* to do with him.

"Weasel?" he asked.

I shook my head, focused on my best friend. Weasel was our code name for the men trying to weasel, quite literally, their way into my pants and then into hers.

I was just about ready to say fuck it—or me, rather—even if Jordan was a Weasel. He smelled amazing. His body was hard and hot against mine.

And it had been way too long since I'd had sex.

"No chemistry on my part—" Seraphina began.

"Your friend isn't who I'm attracted to," Jordan growled out. "You are, and it's fucking pissing me off that you don't believe that."

Bad Breakup
Book Two
www.books2read.com/BadBreakup

CeCe

"You're even more beautiful than I remember," he said, and the rough edges of his accent hacked at the words, making them more of a growl rather than a soft sentiment.

Her breath caught, and she found her eyes drawn to the stormy blue of Colin's.

And she stared again, utterly entranced before she remembered how it had all ended.

Her in a white dress.

Alone, except for the priest who'd given her a pitying look and invited her to stay as long as she needed.

But it had always been like this, Colin's gruff words winning her over. They were unexpected from him—he was typically so reserved and taciturn. And that compliment, freely given as it was, chipped away at any defenses she managed to erect.

The problem was that his words weren't always followed up by action. In fact, they were typically trailed by pain for her and fury for him.

The hurt of those memories—of Colin so angry, her so broken—helped shore up her resolve.

"Don't say things like that," she snapped and started to pop her earbuds back in. Her friends at home had filled her phone with a slew of romantic audiobooks and she decided that she much preferred fictional heroes at the moment.

At least if they broke their heroine's heart, it was only once.

Colin had already broken hers twice.

She wasn't looking for a round three.

—Get your copy at www.books2read.com/BadBreakup.

Bad Husband

Book Three
www.books2read.com/BadHusband

Heather

"I'm getting drunk," he said, but allowed her to pull him inside the car so that her driver could shut the door behind them.

"You're already drunk," she said.

He stiffened. "*More* drunk."

"Fine," she said, half-worried he was going to launch himself from the sedan. She'd never seen Clay like this. Usually he was so cold and uncompromising, impenetrable even under the toughest of negotiations. He was . . . well, he was typically as *Steele*-like as his last name decreed.

She wrapped her arm through his in order to prevent any unplanned exits from the vehicle and gave the driver the name of her favorite bar. "If you really want to drink, let's do it right."

And *then* she'd drop him at his hotel.

Except it didn't happen that way.

Yes, they hit the bar.

Yes, they drank.

Yes, they got plastered.

But then they woke up . . . or at least, *Heather* woke up.

Naked.

With a softly snoring Clay Steele passed out next to her in bed.

That wasn't the worst part.

Because Heather woke up naked and with a softly snoring Clay Steele in her bed *and* she was wearing a giant diamond ring on her left hand.

Still not the worst part.

That came in the form of a slightly crumpled marriage certificate tucked under her right cheek.

And not the one on her face.

She pulled it from beneath her, a cold sweat breaking out on her body, dread in every nerve and cell.

She *still* wasn't prepared for the horror she found.

The marriage license had been signed by . . . Heather O'Keith and Clay Steele.

Holy fuck, what had she done?

—Get your copy at www.books2read.com/BadHusband.

Bad Hookup
Book Four
www.books2read.com/BadHookup

Rachel

The man didn't take the hint. He didn't leave.

Why won't he leave?

She dropped her chin to her chest.

"So," he finally said after another lengthy—and silent— moment. "Gay, taken, or not interested?"

"Oh my God," she moaned, one hand coming up to push her bangs off her forehead. "This is *not* happening."

"I—" A beat then his voice was incredulous. "I *know* that moan." Warm fingers grasped her wrist, tugged until she could see him in all his yumminess.

Her moment of weakness. Her hookup because she'd been feeling desperate and lonely and—

"It's you," he said softly.

Yes, it was *her*. Rachel, the good girl who didn't sleep around, who *certainly* didn't hook up with random strangers in a bar.

Rachel, who *had* hooked up with a stranger.

The sex had been damned good. Incredible, actually.

But it had been just that. Sex. And she hadn't been able to let go of the guilt. She'd now slept with a grand total of two men in her life, and one of them was her husband.

"I—" She tugged at her wrist. "I need to go."

—Get your copy at books2read.com/BadHookup.

Bad Divorce
Book Five
www.books2read.com/BadDivorce

Bec

Bec really didn't expect to see another person waiting for her when the doors opened with a soft *ding* and she stepped off.

But there *was* another person waiting just outside her front door.

A person she never expected to see again.

Luke Pearson.

Her ex-husband.

It was one-fucking-thirty in the morning, and her ex-husband was sitting on the floor outside her apartment.

Asleep.

Fuming, she marched over to him and kicked his shoe. Hard.

"Luke. Why in the ever loving fuck are you here?"

His lids peeled back and sleepy green eyes met hers. "Becky," he murmured. "You're gorgeous as always." The drowsiness began to fade from his expression. "Did you just come from work?" He glanced down at his phone. "Do you know what time it is?"

"Of course I know what time it is—" Bec bit back the words. Fuck, but wasn't this conversation an exact replica of the broken record one they'd had *way* too many times over the course of their relationship?

She crossed her arms. "Never mind that." A glare that had withered balls much bigger than Luke's "Why did you break into my apartment?"

He stood. "First, I didn't break into your apartment. This is the hall. Second," he hurried to say when she opened her mouth to argue semantics, "I didn't break in. You used our anniversary as the code."

Oh for fuck's sake.

Well, she was changing that tomorrow . . . today . . . fuck, *yesterday*, now that—

"Go away, Luke," she said, pushing past him and unlocking her door while blocking his view of the keypad that was identical to that of the elevator. Her front door's code was not the date of her anniversary with her ex.

But Luke probably already knew that, given that he had been sitting on the floor of her hallway rather than on her couch, beer in hand, feet making prints on her glass coffee table.

Men.

Fucking men.

She slammed the door closed behind her and threw the dead bolt. The knock approximately one second later did not surprise her. Bec dropped her briefcase to the floor then opened it just enough to shoot angry eyes at him through the narrow gap the dead bolt allowed.

Serious green eyes fixed onto hers. "We need to talk."

"Luke," she snapped. "I'm exhausted. It's the middle of the

night. I wouldn't have any patience to talk to my best friends right now, let alone my ex-husband."

"Funny story about that," he said, his lips curving. "Turns out that I'm not actually your *ex*-husband."

—Get your copy at www.books2read.com/BadDivorce

———

Bad Fiancé
Book Six
www.books2read.com/BadFiance

Seraphina

Sera was alone, pining after a man who'd created the latest social media craze.

Yup. Her life was *ah-maz-ing*.

Tate cleared his throat, and Sera realized she'd been staring at him dumbfounded for a good couple of minutes.

"How can I help you today?" she asked. "I do hope"—*Do hope? What was she, British? Ugh.*—"I-uh . . . I hope you were able to find a house. The agents I passed along are very good at finding unique properties, and I even gave them a few locations to start with . . . " She bit her lip, attempting to stop the ramble.

"No."

Just no.

Um. Okay.

He lifted a hand, rubbed the back of his neck. The movement made his shirt lift, exposing several inches of flat stomach and tan skin and, oh God, a trail of blond hair leading south. Her mouth watered, desperate to trace that path with her tongue—

Sera sucked in a breath, popped to her feet.

"Ah. I'm sorry." She picked up a random file, pretending to know what was in it. "I'm actually really busy, so this will have to continue another time."

Like never.

She rounded her desk, forced a smile. "Mr. Conner," she said when he didn't move. "I'll have my assistant schedule something soon."

"Seraphina."

She shivered at the sound of her name on his lips—soft, a little raspy, and deep enough to conjure all sorts of unhelpful fantasies in her mind.

Shaking herself, she moved to open the door.

Suddenly, Tate was there, hand on hers, body inches away, spicy scent inundating her senses.

Sera's breath caught. "What are you—?"

He seemed to be arguing with himself then finally, those piercing blue eyes locked onto hers. "I need you to marry me."

—Get your copy at www.books2read.com/BadFiance

Bad Boyfriend
Book Seven
www.books2read.com/BadBoyfriendEF

Seraphina

Sera was alone, pining after a man who'd created the latest social media craze.

Yup. Her life was *ah-maz-ing*.

Tate cleared his throat, and Sera realized she'd been staring at him dumbfounded for a good couple of minutes.

"How can I help you today?" she asked. "I do hope"—*Do*

hope? What was she, British? *Ugh.*—"I-uh . . . I hope you were able to find a house. The agents I passed along are very good at finding unique properties, and I even gave them a few locations to start with . . . " She bit her lip, attempting to stop the ramble.

"No."

Just no.

Um. Okay.

He lifted a hand, rubbed the back of his neck. The movement made his shirt lift, exposing several inches of flat stomach and tan skin and, oh God, a trail of blond hair leading south. Her mouth watered, desperate to trace that path with her tongue—

Sera sucked in a breath, popped to her feet.

"Ah. I'm sorry." She picked up a random file, pretending to know what was in it. "I'm actually really busy, so this will have to continue another time."

Like never.

She rounded her desk, forced a smile. "Mr. Conner," she said when he didn't move. "I'll have my assistant schedule something soon."

"Seraphina."

She shivered at the sound of her name on his lips—soft, a little raspy, and deep enough to conjure all sorts of unhelpful fantasies in her mind.

Shaking herself, she moved to open the door.

Suddenly, Tate was there, hand on hers, body inches away, spicy scent inundating her senses.

Sera's breath caught. "What are you—?"

He seemed to be arguing with himself then finally, those piercing blue eyes locked onto hers. "I need you to marry me."

—Get your copy at www.books2read.com/BadBoyfriendEF

Bad Blind Date
Book Eight
www.books2read.com/BadBlindDate

Trix

Regardless, she was back in California for the time being, ready to begin a new chapter in her life.

Apparently, that meant starting by dating.

At least, that was Heather's logic.

Or maybe Trix's own brand of stupid.

Still, whatever it was that had convinced her to come, she was there now and was going to make the best of it.

Or at least that *had been* her thought until she recognized who was approaching the table.

Him.

Trix slammed her eyes closed and counted to five.

It could *not* be him.

Could not—

She opened her eyes.

Clay was on his feet, shaking the man's hand, shaking *Jet's* hand, and making introductions all around. Heather looked thrilled, probably because Jet was gorgeous and funny and smart—

"And this is Heather's sister, Trix. She's a nurse."

Jet knew that.

Because he knew her. *Intimately.*

The doctor and the nurse. So cliché. So stupid on her part to think that things in her life might have turned out differently.

He'd been smiling as he turned to meet her, and it was almost comical to see his expression darken to fury. Or it *would* have, if that fury hadn't been directed at her. By then his hand was already in hers, mid-shake and *fuck* if his touch didn't still make sparks shoot down her arm.

She went to pull back, but he held fast then jerked her forward, as though he were giving her a hug in greeting.

No one at the table could see that he was hissing in her ear.

"What the fuck are you playing at, Trixie?"

—Get your copy at www.books2read.com/BadBlindDate

ALSO BY ELISE FABER

Billionaire's Club (**all stand alone**)

Bad Night Stand

Bad Breakup

Bad Husband

Bad Hookup

Bad Divorce

Bad Fiancé

Bad Boyfriend

Bad Blind Date

Bad Wedding (July 19th, 2020)

Bad Engagement (October 12th, 2020)

KTS Series

Fire and Ice (Hurt Anthology, stand alone novella)

Riding The Edge

Love, Action, Camera (all stand alone)

Dotted Line

Action Shot

Close-Up

End Scene

Love After Midnight (**all stand alone**)

Rum and Notes

Virgin Daiquiri

On The Rocks (Sept 27th, 2020)

Gold Hockey (**all stand alone**)

Blocked

Backhand

Boarding

Benched

Breakaway

Breakout

Checked

Coasting

Centered

Life Sucks Series (**all stand alone**)

Train Wreck

Hot Mess (August 3rd, 2020)

Roosevelt Ranch Series (**all stand alone, series complete**)

Disaster at Roosevelt Ranch

Heartbreak at Roosevelt Ranch

Collision at Roosevelt Ranch

Regret at Roosevelt Ranch

Desire at Roosevelt Ranch

Phoenix Series (**read in order**)

Phoenix Rising

Dark Phoenix

Phoenix Freed

Phoenix: LexTal Chronicles (rereleasing soon, stand alone, Phoenix world)

From Ashes

In Flames

To Smoke

Stand Alones

Someday, Maybe (YA)

ABOUT THE AUTHOR

USA Today bestselling author, Elise Faber, loves chocolate, Star Wars, Harry Potter, and hockey (the order depending on the day and how well her team -- the Sharks! -- are playing). She and her husband also play as much hockey as they can squeeze into their schedules, so much so that their typical date night is spent on the ice. Elise changes her hair color more often than some people change their socks, loves sparkly things, and is the mom to two exuberant boys. She lives in Northern California. Connect with her in her Facebook group, the Fabinators or find more information about her books at www.elisefaber.com.

facebook.com/elisefaberauthor

amazon.com/author/elisefaber

bookbub.com/profile/elise-faber

instagram.com/elisefaber

goodreads.com/elisefaber

pinterest.com/elisefaberwrite

Made in the USA
Middletown, DE
04 March 2021